Special Agent Kandice

SPECIAL AGENT KANDICE

Mimi Barbour

Sarna Publishing

Special Agent Kandice

The Undercover FBI Series – Book 4

Contents

Dedication

I wanted to dedicate this book to everyone who has health issues they're dealing with. It's a scary, horrible time to live through and my heart goes out to you. Just know you're not alone.

***

In particular, I wanted to mention Joan, one of my dearest friends. She's not a person I see a lot, but when I do, I adore her. She has the sweetness of Kandice... and the same internal toughness to fight the health battle she's in right now. The world needs more people like her so I pray she stays with us for a long time to come.

Acknowledgements

First, I want to thank **Neil Low**, a Seattle Police Captain, who has kindly been my go-to person for the specifics on weapons – of which I have no knowledge. Plus, details on bank robberies and how law enforcement might deal with this issue.

Neil is a wonderful author is his own right – his latest book released called "Deadly Attraction" is a great read. See his website here.

Next, I wanted to mention how thankful I am to my many wonderful Beta Readers. I rely on them a great deal to give me feedback, catch editing errors and write reviews that are so necessary before a book can be promoted.

Last, but not least, I want to thank my family who put up with me always walking around with my head in the clouds... plotting my next story. XO

Praise

"Kandi has a way about her that draws people to her; her heart is so big, it's hard for her to sound like a tough FBI Agent, but she tries. Kandi is well suited to her job as a crisis negotiator. When their office gets a new ASAC, Dan Black, Kandi feels drawn to him and doesn't really understand why, as Dan seems not to like her from the moment they meet. Dan was supposedly demoted from AD of the Criminal Investigation Division in Washington and sent to this Seattle Branch of the FBI. He had forgotten Kandi was assigned to the same office. Now he's in trouble! This is really a heartwarming love story with an interesting "cops and robbers" storyline!" ~ *reviewed by Susan*

"Can't wait to read more by this author. This was the first book I read by this author so my expectations weren't too much, but they should have been. I really enjoyed this book. I can't wait to read more of her books. I even joined her newsletter." ~ *reviewed by SusieQ*

"In my opinion, the Special Agent series by Mimi Barbour just keeps getting better and better. I loved this story, the humor, the characters and the plot...especially the things I didn't see coming.

Wonderfully entertaining read!" ~ *reviewed by Anne C*

Also author of...

— Action–Packed Thrillers! —
Vegas Series – Complete Boxed Set
Partners (Book 1)
Roll the Dice (Book 2)
Vegas Shuffle (Book 3)
High Stakes Gamble (Book 4)
Spin the Wheel (Book 5)
Let it Ride (Book 6)
***

Undercover FBI Series
— Popular & Compelling! —
Special Agent Francesca (Book 1)
Special Agent Finnegan (Book 2)
Special Agent Maximilian (Book 3)
Special Agent Kandice (Book 4)
Special Agent Booker (Book 5)
Special Agent Charli (Book 6 to be released July 2018)
***

Holiday Heartwarmers Trilogy
— Truly a Christmas favorite! —
Holiday Heartwarmers Series
Please Keep Me (Book 1)
Snow Pup (Book 2)
Find Me a Home (Book 3)
Frosty the Snowman (Book 4)
Love of my Life (Book 5)
***

Mob Tracker Series
— She's unstoppable! —

Unforgettable Suspense (Multi-author Box Set)
Unforgettable Danger (Multi-author Box Set)
Unforgettable Trouble (Multi-author Box Set)
Unforgettable Weddings (Multi-author Box Set)
A Wedding She'll Remember (Multi-author Box Set)
Enchanted Romances (Multi-author Box Set)
Sweet and Sassy Brides (Multi-author Box Set)
Love, Christmas 2 (Multi-author Box Set)

~*~*~*~

All Mimi's books can be found on her Amazon Author Page:
OR
Website: http://mimibarbour.com

Chapter One

"Smile at me one more time with those gleaming pearly-whites, and I'm liable to smash them down your throat. You got it?" Special Agent Kandice Warner had just arrived at the FBI office and greeted her co-worker.

Some of the other staffers who'd been watching laughed. One clapped, and the agent Kandice had been directing her threat to gloomily shook his head. "Kandi, what's with the compliment? And your eyes are friggin' twinkling. You gotta look like you mean it. God-almighty, sweets, it wasn't at all believable."

Hands on her hips, posing, Kandi grouched, "I practiced that for half an hour. What was wrong with it this time?"

"Well, first of all, your eyes were soft, you got too damn close, and when you're sarcastic to a perp, ya just don't pat his arm."

Laughter rang out in the main room where a dozen or so others worked. Catcalls and whistles followed. One voice was louder and could be heard over the rest. "Kandi just doesn't have the personality of a Pitbull, Wesley. She's our sweetheart."

"Yeah, man, leave her alone. It's bad enough that we're a bunch of hardened agents. We like her just the way she is."

Wesley Snow, chubby with longish hair, glasses that never stayed up and a friendly disposition, snarled to the others, "Hell, this isn't my idea. Kandi insists she needs to learn how to be scary, like the rest of us."

Horrified, Kandi jumped in. "I never said that, you goofball. I said I wanted the criminals to take me more seriously. Not to decide they can run when I have a gun pointed at them."

This brought more laughter and Kandi, not having the heart to continue with her snit, giggled with them.

"Give it up, sweetheart. We'll look after you, same as we bin doin' since forever. You're like our mascot." Bobbi, her best friend, came over and wrapped her in a hug, her brown eyes softening and her darkish-coffee skin glowing with health and vitality. The warmth, the smell of her vanilla body lotion, even the ruffling she gave Kandi's curls, should have given Kandi a soft feeling. And it did... But the dissatisfaction still hovered and wouldn't fade.

"I can't let it go, Bobbi. They have to start believing I'm competent, or my credibility goes right out the window."

Bobbi nodded, her hand now holding one of Kandi's. "Look, the reason that asshole ran away from you yesterday wasn't because you didn't scare him enough to follow orders. You were cool and said most of the words I would have used." The rest of her co-workers nodded.

"I did?" Kandi knew they all considered Bobbi a level-headed agent who came off as being one not to mess with. *Maybe this isn't so bad after all.*

"Hell, yeah." A male voice added.

"S'truth." Wesley nodded and joined in.

"Then why did he wink at me and run away?"

"'Cause you were smiling beseechingly, and you made one small mistake... I never say, *please* stop."

Kandi lowered her head in disgust. "I did say that, didn't I? He knew I'd never shoot him."

"Honey, no matter how good you were in training, or how thorough you are when it comes to talking these assholes down in a crisis negotiation, you don't have the killer instinct."

"I guess you're right." Kandi pushed her hands through her headful of blonde curls that bounced every which way and grinned sadly. "I'm nothing but a wuss."

"Oh, no, honey. That's not what I said. Why, we've watched you stand up to some of the meanest sons-a-bitches ever and you never back down. By the time you're finished with the pricks, you have them following you like puppy-dogs, willing to do whatever you say. It's uncanny. I wish I had your talent."

The rest of the room muttered various agreements, until their new boss entered and ended everyone's fun.

Kandi watched the room settle down, busy agents now avidly working, typing and making phone calls. She caught Wesley's wink before his head went down too.

This guy scared the stuffing out of all of them. He had the coldest disposition of anyone Kandi had ever met. His reputation preceded him, and the fact that he'd been demoted from his hoity-toity position in Washington, as the Assistant Director of the Criminal Investigative Division, to the lowly Seattle branch as an Assistant Special Agent in Charge must have been very demoralizing for the man whose gritty personality terrified them.

Not that anyone had the guts or the stupidity to bring it up when he'd arrived yesterday. Fred More, the SAC, had accompanied him into their office and made the introductions.

"I'm sure we were all sorry to see Neil Ware

leave, but that old agent put in his time and deserved his retirement. So, I'm pleased to introduce you to the man we've chosen to take his place, ASAC Dan Black."

Most of the team had been happy to see Neil leave for various reasons. Kandi had wished him well and a happy retirement, but the others were glad to be done with the snarky, exacting asshole. Now they had a different man to deal with. And he looked to be worse.

Standing next to his latest assistant, Fred had looked short, plain and insignificant. Prior to that, Kandi would have described the SAC as six feet tall, nice-looking and obviously in authority, but the new man had a way of overshadowing other males in his vicinity.

Though Fred had been somewhat ingratiating when he'd said his piece and hurried from the room, his final remark rang in the quiet. "Dan Black knows more than most of you put together so work hard for him, follow his instructions and make us proud."

Left alone with the dark-haired stunner, his expensive gray suit making every other man in the room look dowdy, Kandi's colleagues had shuffled nervously.

Expecting the man to say a few words of greeting, make an effort to reach out to his people, Kandi, and everyone else, was robbed. As they were introduced, he shook their hands, studied each person for a few seconds. At the end of the introductions, he nodded and left them all standing there while he disappeared into his new office.

Uncomfortable, wondering why he'd stared at her the longest, Kandi mourned their old boss. Feeling mean, she wanted Neil to enjoy his retirement but, contradictorily, she also wished him back at work.

Dan Black's eyes had been cold and uncompromising, digging into soft places she only shared with people she liked. And he certainly wasn't one of them. Okay, she had no reason for this aversion she felt. In fact, he had her total deference as a co-worker, a boss she would be working for.

Was he familiar? Did he remind her of someone? She ignored her misgivings.

Of course, there had to be respect. But she'd hold off on her final verdict until she got to know him better. Added to that, when and if he ever stopped making her nervous, or leaving her trembling like a schoolgirl with a crush on the new boy in class, then... and only then, would she decide to let him in.

Once he'd disappeared behind his glass walls, like everyone else, she'd gone to her own cubicle with its old-fashioned separators which only measured half-way to the ceiling. Head down, she began filling in some of the endless reports while she had the chance.

But before getting too involved, she leaned over the wall, saw Bobbi on the phone and mouthed "Lunch", and smiled when Bobbi empathically nodded. Then she sat back down and went to work.

In her job as the FBI's only Crisis Negotiator in the area, one never knew when the next call would come. Thankfully, it had been a quiet morning and they'd gotten a lot done.

Because Bobbi got a callout about an ongoing case, they never did get their lunch together. Kandi just spent the day at her desk.

Her only complaint was that every time she looked up, her gaze automatically lifted forward, and it was just her luck to be in Dan Black's direct path. Utterly nerve-wracked to find his eyes on her each time, she smiled with her lips only and resumed work. It had been a long day.

***

Wesley, glasses halfway down his nose, broke into her reverie, "Kandi, we're on. There's a hostage situation at a downtown bank. Ten people are being held, two kids." Bobbi put her phone down and leapt to her feet. She went to Dan's door and gave him a brief rundown, while the rest of the team grabbed their equipment and headed to the SWAT vehicles.

Kids! Blast it! Kandi hated seeing children involved in these types of crimes. Her heart filling with its usual soft squishiness, she sought her weapon and followed the group. The last person she expected to tag along was their new boss.

Chapter Two

After meeting his new crew, ASAC Dan Black had gone into his new office and collapsed in his chair. For the first time in his life, his legs had weakened and were threatening to crumble.

It was her! Goddammit... he knew it. No one else could have those sparkling, vivid blue eyes, of that particular shade. A mix between—hell, he didn't know. Blue should be fucking blue. But, in her case it wasn't. Instead her eyes might be described as unusual, captivating... irresistible. Eyes that lit up like they had their own intense sun shining inside her head. They grabbed a person and sucked them in.

He should know. Blasted hell... back in the dark days of his youth, when he'd hated everyone, she'd been the only person in the world who could draw a smile from him and lift his spirits.

For almost a year, they'd ridden the same bus in Seattle, her to a pricey private facility run by the nuns, and him to a public, moldy, rodent-infested torture chamber they called school.

He'd been in the eighth grade, thirteen years old, an unhappy, mixed-up boy. His nightmare of a dysfunctional home had turned him into a hardened creature even then, and those experiences had left a chip on his shoulder that still fit there well today.

He glanced over at her and saw she'd been staring his way. Did she recognize him?

Nah! She hadn't. He'd known right away. She'd given him the lovely smile of a stranger who wanted to like you, but who was waiting for you to give them a reason to do so.

He'd ignored the invitation and had probed her in the same way he did with most folks. Except, most folks didn't leave him wanting to grin like an idiot or hold onto a warm hand that had soft skin which left a Taser-zapping jolt.

Shit! Now what the hell was he going to do? He needed to keep his head straight on this mission. He'd promised his boss, his best friend and mentor, to squirrel out the informant; the one they'd discovered was working out of the Seattle office. But that was before he'd realized she'd be in the same department. Last time he'd allowed himself to read her file, and call in a few favors, he'd had her assigned to a desk... a nice safe place for the soft-hearted female he cared about.

Back in Washington, Director Bob Mires had come to him with the special request to work undercover because the husband of his beloved niece, Wesley Snow, could be the possible culprit.

Since the Assistant to the Special Agent in Charge, Neil Ware, was retiring, they had the perfect opportunity for Dan to step in without any suspicion.

"Dan, I hate to ask this of you, but I trust you to keep this between us. You were raised in Seattle and would know your way around. If you were to be disciplined for an invented screw-up, it's feasible that we would demote you, and you might request a move back to your old home town."

"Hey, Bob! I'm due some leave—"

"Leave? You workaholic prick, you've racked up so much time off, we'd be screwed if you ever took it all at once."

"No worries about that. Look, Ryan, my assistant, can look after things here for the foreseeable future. I'm good to go. What kind of information is being weaseled out of the office?"

"Drug cartel stuff mostly. Two of our agents have been killed while undercover. An informant, one of our own, the worst kind of prick imaginable, has given info over to the gangs acquiring large shipments. Our men were played, fed false data that they passed on, then shot and left as a message for the bureau."

"Yeah! I read about it earlier this week. It's utter bullshit."

"I know. Look, it's been kept under wraps because we have other boys in the field. If this crap continues, we'll have to pull everyone else in. But then we'll have lost any hold we have on the meth and H that floods the city. And... spreads all over the mid-west."

"What makes you think your niece's husband could be the culprit?"

"I don't." Bob stood and waved his hands like he always did when he was agitated. "Hell, I don't. But they're watching all the incoming and outgoing messages on everyone's phones, having the IT boys sneaking through everyone's computers. It's a senseless waste of time. None of our guys would be so stupid as to use the company's electronics."

"But...?"

"Wesley has had a few messages that look a bit suspect. He's e-mailed one of the people we know in the Cortés gang. They're the biggest cartel we know of in that area and all our leads trace back to them shooting our agent. Look, the files are all here. Read everything and let me know what you think." Bob handed Dan a thumb drive and watched as he put it in his inner jacket pocket.

"Glad to. And, Bob... we both know that just because Snow's been in touch with one of the known criminals doesn't make him dirty. Remember, life is stranger than fiction. You taught me that. It could be a purely innocent exchange."

"I really hope so. My niece Patti dotes on the bastard. Let's hope her people skills have improved from her college days."

Dan smiled, remembering the photograph Bob had shown him of the short-haired, bubbly redhead who Bob's brother and his wife, Sarah, had raised. He hoped so too.

"I'll look after this, Bob. I promise. Set the wheels in motion and let's get the show on the road." Little did he know then, he'd be facing the only female in the world he'd stalked since he'd joined the bureau but had purposely kept his distance from.

Chapter Three

A day later and Dan still felt like he'd been punched in the gut by tenacious memories with a vicious sense of humor.

Watching her arrive yesterday had set him off. Then, listening to her joking with her colleagues had made him smile, but that was before she'd gotten close enough for her magic to infect him again.

This morning, he'd purposely stayed hidden in his office, not trusting that his brimming hunger wouldn't jump into his eyes and she'd see the need.

Pulled from his reveries by a figure approaching, Dan spotted the slightly chubby man pushing his sliding glasses back in place. *No way you're dirty!*

Snow looked like a straight-shooter to him, but

one never knew. This curly-haired prick didn't seem the type to be an informant. But if he was, he'd wish he'd never been born.

He let Snow wait for a few minutes to watch his reaction. Would he fumble, and fidget... get nervous.

He didn't.

"Come in."

"We're off, boss. A bank holdup in the city. They have hostages, ten adults and two kids."

Dan didn't say that Bobbi had already cued him in. Instead, he stood and moved from behind the desk. "Let's go."

Chapter
Four

Situated on a busy street, in the middle of the block, the bank had been cordoned off, people forced behind barriers and there were police cars at each corner to stop traffic. Everyone in the area was being evacuated from the nearest buildings and guided by uniforms to safety.

News vans were being held back by the harassed police, and the media nutcases were remorseless in trying to get closer, sneak through the barriers.

As they approached, the deputy at the scene looked a mite panicked. "We called you guys in because there's one dead and ten others unaccounted for. We were lucky enough to grab some footage of the gang before they shot out the street cam. Turns out, the perps showed up on your most-wanted list."

Before Wesley or Bobbi could ask the question, Dan Black appeared on the scene and asked it instead. "Who are they?"

Kandice stepped aside to let Dan take over. Normally, she, or one of her crew, would be asking for answers. But no one here would be arguing the right of leadership with the black-haired, vest-wearing dude with a badge showing his qualifications as the ASAC.

Instinctively, obviously knowing leadership when it appeared, the deputy turned his way. "It looks like the Dixon brothers are at it again. This time, we have Samuel, Paul and Adam. From what we've learned, Adam's girl tagged along also. Haven't got a make on her yet, but according to a witness from across the street, she was draped all over him before they entered the bank."

"Where's the witness?"

"Mrs. Witherspoon. We're holding her in the Walgreens across the street. We've set up a temporary control center in there."

"Fine. We'll be working from the FBI's mobile center from now on, but we'll need to talk with her. Any other witnesses who can give us descriptions?"

"No one else has come forward. Most people don't pay any attention. Everyone's too busy looking at their cell phones or minding their own business. Damn people nowadays—"

Knowing this deputy's penchant for talking, Kandice broke in and began her questions. "Officer Harvey, have you called for the floor plans for the bank and the two surrounding buildings?"

"Not yet, been too busy cordoning off the area and clearing the folks. You know, one of the men got really pissy with me, wanted to go into the clothing store next door to get new pants. Said he didn't think bullets would be able to penetrate concrete walls. Can you believe it?"

Before responding, Kandice had nodded at Bobbi and Wesley, and knowing the routine, Bobbi answered, "We're on it, Cupcake. We'll find a way into the building. Or at least, get eyes on the scene."

Uncomfortable with Bobbi's unconscious use of her nickname, Kandi just sighed, and since Agent Black didn't step up, she continued. "You say one person is dead."

Officer Harvey looked at Dan as he replied. "Yeah, looks like the bank manager set off the alarm and was caught. They shot him and threw him out on the sidewalk. We shielded a couple of the officers who retrieved his body, but it was too late. The man was dead, one bullet in the forehead... vicious sons-a-bitches."

Kandi added, "All seven brothers are psychotic, but the baby of the family, Adam, is the worst. He's a maniac, crazy over anything in skirts, but plays rough. We caught him last year for statutory rape of a minor, but she backed off and refused to testify after his brothers paid her family a visit. Killed her mother, raped her older sister and left her younger brother a paraplegic. We've been after these boys for one heck of a long time."

Bobbi reappeared. "Kandi, we've got a call. Are you ready to negotiate? They want to talk to the boss."

Before she could answer, Dan broke in. "I'll be taking the call, Agent Carter."

Smiling, Bobbi answered, "Please, just Bobbi."

"Agent Bobbi." Dan whirled around and stopped when Kandice stepped in his path.

Kandice didn't know if he had been joking with Bobbi or putting her in her place. His expression hadn't changed one iota, still grim — the ruthlessness apparent for everyone to see.

"Sir, I'm the Chief Negotiator and will need to assess the situation properly. I can only do that by talking to the perp."

"Not this time, Agent Warner. I read up on these guys, and they don't play games. They won't fall for your particular style of charm. Fact is, they'd shoot their own mother if she stood in their way. But I'd appreciate you talking with the witness, Mrs. Witherspoon, and any input you might have otherwise."

His eyes drilled into hers and she saw the inflexibility. The man would be doing her job, and there wasn't a damn thing she could do about it.

Chapter Five

The woman, waiting to give evidence, looked fidgety, anxious to be away from the crime scene, and Kandice couldn't blame her. In her forties, a bit of a food addict, the chubby lady had sweat pools showing under the arms on her too-tight red T-shirt, and her frizzy, dirty-blonde hair needed another perm. But to Kandi, the bravery of a person who was willing to step forward always brought pleasure and she let the poor woman feel her softer side.

Holding out her hand, she said, "Hello, Mrs. Witherspoon. I'm Special Agent Warner." Pointing to Bobbi, she added, "And this is Special Agent Carter. We're with the FBI SWAT team and would like to ask you a few questions."

Shaking hands with each of the agents seemed to make the witness feel more respected, and she straightened in her chair. "Like I told the other cops... ah, officers, it was the kiss that caught my attention. The two were deep into it, tongues, the whole lot and in the middle of the street — disgusting. It made me stop 'cause kids were on the sidewalk. And they was watchin' and sniggerin' too."

Showing her the images that Bobbi had printed out of all seven members of the Dixon family, Kandi let the witness look at each before asking her question. "Can you say for sure which of these men was part of the group that went into the bank?"

"Oh, sure. These two were laughin' and pushing at each other." Mrs. Witherspoon pointed at Samuel and Paul. Then she picked up the mug shot of Adam, glanced at it carefully and threw the page away from her, repulsed. "And he's lover-boy."

Kandice smiled to show her appreciation and watched Mrs. Witherspoon visually relax and smile back, then swipe at the perspiration on her forehead. "Can we get you anything, ma'am? Coffee, a soft drink?"

"Yes, please, a diet coke would be great."

Kandice nodded at one of the agents nearby, grinned and watched him point at the others in the room to take orders from them also.

"Now, can you tell us anything about the girl? Her age, hair coloring, clothes—whatever you remember that sticks out."

"She was maybe twenty, had long red hair and wore short shorts. Her T-shirt ended just below her boobs... ah, breasts, probably to show off the tattoos on her stomach. She had 'em on her right arm too. Like a dragon or a big snake. If'n you ask me, the girl wore way too much make-up, tryin' to look like a movie star."

Kandice took the distorted image they'd taken off the street cam and held it up. "Is this her?"

"Yeah! That's the girl."

"You live just a couple of streets over, in one of the apartments at the back of the laundry, right?"

"Right. My husband and I run the sweat shop. Damn hot work, but what can you do? Gotta pay the bills. Know what I mean?"

"Yes, ma'am. I sure do." Kandice smiled, patted the woman's clenched hand and watched her relax. "Can you tell me if you've ever seen her around this area before? I mean, you must know a lot of people from customers that you serve."

"Yeah, you're right there. But she's not familiar to me at all."

"Okay then, here's the officer with your drink. Mrs. Witherspoon, you've been a huge help." Kandice handed over one of her cards. "If you think of anything else, please call me."

Kandice stood to leave, just as the sound of a bullet ripped through the air. For a big woman, Kandice had never seen anyone move so fast. Mrs. Witherspoon now lay spread-eagled and quivering

on the floor, with a pool of dark liquid gurgling out
of the upended can by her side.

Chapter Six

As they raced around the safety zone to get to the Mobile Command Center they usually worked from, Bobbi beat Kandi to the back door and held it open.

Entering, they saw two of their fellow workers beside Wesley and Dan sitting at the computers, everyone working, heads down. All the men had removed their suit jackets and were wearing the requisite Kevlar vests, the same as Kandice and Bobbi wore.

"What's up?" she asked before Bobbi had a chance.

Wesley looked pleased to see them. "They won't talk to anyone. Crazy bastards say they'll just wait for their brothers to break 'em out."

Bobbi laughed. "What, they think their brothers are superheroes or something?"

"Who knows what those psychopaths have in their heads. Agent Black just offered to negotiate, and while he was talking to them they shot Melissa Knowles, one of the women."

Kandice stepped forward. "You got eyes?"

"Yep. The boys ran the wiring through the hot air ducts. We can see into the front of the bank where they're holding the hostages, and into the back office where they've stacked the money waiting to get out. Silly bastards think they still have a chance."

"Why'd they shoot Melissa then?"

"Seems she pissed them off. Wanted to take her daughter to the toilet and they wouldn't let her."

"Show me." Kandice sat at an empty screen and watched the replay of the events as they happened. As was her habit, she talked as she watched. "Paul didn't like Adam doing that; see his face. He's uncomfortable. And the girlfriend, she turned away. Something's fishy about her. Watch her hand there. Rewind it for a few seconds, Wes. There. Now watch her hand."

Sure enough, the chick had moved away from Adam and her hands had lifted as if she wanted to stop her boyfriend from pulling the trigger. Instantly she recovered, but it was a telling move, and Kandice had worked with less than that before. "She's sympathetic. See, she's turned away now. Look, she's squaring her shoulders. That girl is most definitely not who she seems to be."

Dan came and looked over her shoulder. "You're right. She's not hardened to this sort of behavior. Zoom in, Agent Snow. Look! She's actually terrified but hiding it. Good call, Agent Warner."

Uncomfortable at his formality, Kandice ignored his compliment. Instead, she asked a point-blank question. "Can you run back the tape of your conversation for me?"

Dan nodded at Wesley, who replayed the audio while they all listened. Kandi heard music in the background like they were having a party. "Yeah?" The voice grated, as if the owner was suffering from laryngitis or had just had a bad coughing spell.

Then she heard Dan. "This is Agent Dan Black with the FBI. Can I talk to the person in charge over there so we can get this situation dealt with in an expedient manner and in the safest way for everyone?"

"Hey, asshole. You're talking to him. Whaddaya want?"

"In case you haven't realized, we have you and your brothers completely penned in, Mr. Dixon. Every exit is covered, and all we want is to settle this dispute with as little harm done as possible."

A harsh laugh followed and then a coughing fit. Finally, the voice answered. "Wait—I'll just go put on my I-give-a-fuck hat, Mr. FBI-man. We have family who'll look after our escape, so don't you worry your promotion-ambitious little head about things that don't concern you."

Kandi had cottoned on to the superior tone in Dan's voice and had no doubt that Sam heard it also. "It's no problem at all. Tell us what we can do for you."

There was a grunt followed by a long-drawn-out chuckle with no humor whatsoever. "I know just what you want to do for us.... Adam, leave the bitch alone. Oh, for Chrissakes."

The call was severed, and the dial tone drowned out the horrific gunshot and screams that had followed.

Bobbi broke the silence. "Bastards!"

Wes got their attention. "You might want to watch this now."

They returned to the real-time screening and saw that the hostages were all forced together, huddling on the floor in a group around Melissa. They'd been placed in the bank's main customer area.

Now catatonic, shock rendering her inert, Melissa's small daughter, in the arms of an older woman who cuddled her, had wet herself, her white pants discolored and damp.

One of the younger women, maybe sixteen or so, had removed her blouse and used it to wrap around the wound on Melissa's shoulder. With only a skimpy camisole to cover her young voluptuousness, the girl ignored the criminals and focused on helping the poor victim.

Samuel stepped into view. He had lank, longish blond hair and was dressed in black jeans and a black leather denim jacket over a white-turned-to-gray T-shirt. The MK47 hanging from his hand, ready to be lifted in a moment's notice, promised him instant respect.

They watched as he reached into his upper pocket and withdrew a cigarette package. Clearly, they saw he only had two cigarettes left. His face turned mean when it dawned on him he'd be running out soon.

He stashed the package roughly back into his pocket without taking one. "Adam, I said leave your bitch alone, and just maybe you could watch these idiots without shooting anyone else."

Taking for granted his little brother would listen, Samuel stomped over to the open vault where his middle brother, Paul, looked after emptying as many of the safety deposit boxes as possible.

First, Paul had forced the terrified head teller to use her master key. After she'd finished, he'd operated a special drill, releasing the lock. If the contents strewn on the floor told the truth, quite a few had been opened.

Suddenly, he lifted the lid of the most recently freed box and a stack of bills appeared — all hundreds. Laughing, he pushed them into the nearby satchel and motioned for the dark-haired, frightened-as-hell clerk to open the one he pointed at.

Sam beamed. "Keep it up, Paul. We need all the cash we can get outta this job. Only hurry. The boys will be here to get us out soon."

Paul stopped his labor. "You sure the stones are in this bank? I've opened almost all the boxes with a thirty-two number. There aren't that many."

"I know what I overheard. The day I opened our safety deposit box while casing the joint, the two women were in front of me in the lineup. Their voices were muffled, but I could have sworn the old bat said thirty-two. She had a purple satin sack of jewels. She said they were diamonds and she intended to deposit them in her personal box. When her daughter asked which one, she told her that number. Guess when you're that rich you need more than one. Remember, I was behind them in the line-up and maybe only caught those two numbers. Just keep checking any box that has them."

Paul scratched his head, still questioning. "What makes you think they're worth all this effort, Sam? I mean a few thousand to some people... hell, that's a lot."

"Hey bro, I'm not some chump-idiot here. Not only were those two decked out in expensive clothes, Coach handbags and dressed all fancy-like in quality gear, but the younger bitch actually said, *I'm glad, Mommy. Having those diamonds at the house made me nervous. Imagine if anyone had broken in and found the safe. What would we have done?"* Sam changed his normally raspy sound to a high-pitched girlish tone before he broke out coughing. Finally, the spasms stopped and he added. "Ha! I almost laughed in their stupid faces."

Meanwhile, Paul giggled like a fool and pushed the white-faced, nervous clerk to move to the next box which had the number thirty-two showing. "I'll keep checking. In the meantime, you'd better watch Adam. Don't know why you said he could come along. Since he met up with that broad yesterday, she's all that's been on his mind. When he showed up here this afternoon with her tagging along, I could have shot him myself, the stupid bugger. What possessed him to bring her?"

"Who the fuck knows. Just keep your cool, bro. I depend on you." Without thinking Sam pulled out his cigarette package and lit one up. Taking a long pull, he blew out the smoke and turned back to see Adam had his chick pinned against the wall.

"For shit's sake, Adam, I'm not gonna tell you again. Let her alone and pay attention to the job. Have you searched the hostages yet?"

Everyone could see the disgust on Sam's face when Adam stopped kissing the struggling woman he'd cruelly crushed against the wall and looked vacantly at his older brother.

"You stupid shit! Go and make sure you get all their purses, wallets and phones now!" Sam roared his orders, his finger pointing at the clustered mass of terrified victims, who were frenzied in their haste to hold up the very items he had mentioned.

Wes cussed under his breath, but he'd only said what the others watching felt too.

Kandi pushed away from the screen. "I need to get in there."

"No way in hell." Dan glared at her and reached for the phone. "I'll attempt another connection. Maybe we can work something out."

"He won't even talk to you. You're a man and, whether you know it or not, you push his buttons. At a time like this, he doesn't need to be strutting his stuff against a male competitor like an elephant seal on the beach. He needs to be wooed."

Kandi had to push this. She knew it would only be a matter of time before Adam noticed what they'd all witnessed on the screen. That the sixteen-year-old's body would tempt any man. Adam wouldn't pass her up. No way. Especially now that he'd been pulled off his girl.

"Let me try. If I can get Sam to admit he has needs, maybe he'll be open to a deal. Like some hostages for cigarettes and food. We want to keep him as calm as possible, and we need to get Melissa some medical attention; she's losing a lot of blood. Plus, her daughter's in a bad way."

Dan looked from face to nodding face, and if he didn't sense the antagonism he'd have to be a fool. Kandi knew that every person in that room, all who'd worked with her on numerous jobs, wanted her in charge of the negotiations. Chances were, it would be their only hope of getting those people out alive.

Chapter
Seven

Dan knew when he'd been cornered with no options other than to pull rank. After all, this was Kandice's job, her speciality if you liked, and her numbers were incredible. He'd read all the recent reports of her negotiating tactics, the risks she'd taken and the amount of times she'd succeeded in winning. The figures spoke for themselves. She knew her job and did it exceedingly well.

"Fine! But I know your habit of offering to replace hostages and that isn't happening here." Just the thought sent his blood pressure soaring and he felt the flush all over his body. *Keep it cool, man. She's just another co-worker. You only met her yesterday.*

"I never know what to expect from these crazies,

sir. I just play the game." She nodded at Wes and waited for him to hand her the phone.

They all watched the screen as Sam strode over to the phone and lifted the receiver. He bellowed, "Whatcha want this time?"

"We heard a shot. Is everyone okay in there?" Kandi's voice could have softened the orneriest of men. Her low feminine tones were incredibly caring.

Instantly, Sam's attitude transformed. "Yeah, sugar. One of the guns went off accidently. Turns out, we killed a plant."

Kandi laughed; humor appeared in her voice though none was visible on her features. "Uh, huh, *sugar*. I can't believe any of you boys are that careless. Hope none of the hostages are hurt."

"Why would you automatically assume we'd shoot a hostage?"

"Cause I very much doubt if you'd shoot each other."

"Ha! You're pretty smart for a cop."

"You're right. That's because I'm not a cop. I'm FBI, Agent Kandice Warner."

"Ah... the Feds. Bet your friends call you Kandi."

"And you'd be correct again. Now, what may I call you?"

"You can call me sugar or Sam. Your choice."

"Then Sam it is."

"I kinda liked sugar better."

Again, Kandi laughed. "Then you'll have to earn

it."

Dan couldn't believe how quickly Kandi had gotten through to the perp and had him eating out of her hands. He looked over at Bobbi and Wes and watched them grin at each other as they high-fived.

"Earn it? How does that work?"

"If you have anyone hurt in there, we can trade that person for whatever you may need. I know you're expecting your brothers to come and rescue you, I heard the replay of your conversation with Agent Black. But in the meantime, you might be needing some supplies. If so, we'll bring you whatever you want for an exchange."

"An exchange. Sugar, are you talking about our prisoners?"

"Of course!" Her tone made it sound like he'd been a genius to catch on. "You have how many in there? We know there were seven bank personnel, but we haven't any information on the numbers of customers."

In reality, they had a pretty good idea from the earlier videos but hadn't received the exact count until one of the cops had brought them the text message a husband had just gotten from his wife. There were eleven captives, which brought the total to eighteen, plus four gang members.

"It's pretty hot in here now. I'm guessing you turned off the air conditioning."

"Didn't you expect us to?"

He laughed. "Sure did."

"Make you a deal. We'll turn it back on if you send out some of those folks. The youngest, any injured, maybe the ones that will give you the most trouble."

"How many are you talking about?"

"Hey, Sam. You know greedy little ol' me. I'd like 'em all, but I'm willing to listen to your suggestion."

Dan liked the interplay and knew she'd thrown the ball back in his court because it was important to let the perp feel they were always in control.

"I'll think on it and get back to you."

"I'll be waiting... sugar. Just hit the reply button and I'll be here."

Everyone heard his chuckle and watched the pleased grin he wore before he broke connection.

Wes started laughing, the sound of relief evident in his tone. "He's willing to play. I hope he got the hint about sending out the young chick. He knows his brother well."

They watched as Sam glanced over at Adam. His younger brother had just noticed Mandy, the sixteen-year-old they were able to place as Mandy Whitford. Her panicked parents had called in as soon as they'd heard the news that the bank she'd been going to was now in a crisis situation.

Holding his breath, anxiety building, craving to walk over to the building and shoot the horny son-of-a-bitch, Dan watched Adam's antics, along with the rest of the gang.

"What do we have here?" Adam snatched Mandy's arm and hauled her closer. "Aren't you a pretty little thang?"

Before Sam could intervene, Adam's girlfriend dove at Mandy, her fists flailing as she attacked. "Bitch. You leave my man alone." She actually pushed Mandy away from Adam and got right into her face. Shoving her back so she ended up scurrying and hiding behind a couple of the men in the group who shielded her with their bodies, she added, "Stupid whore. Idiot! Look at you!"

Kandi pointed at the screen. "Stop it there. Zoom in. She winked."

Bobbi leaned in and agreed. "It's true. What the hell is going on?"

"She's saving her from Adam. Look, the kid's picking up on her hint."

Mandy's straggly long hair now covered her face, tears and snot ran down her cheeks, and her big eyes, enlarged further with fright, did give her the appearance of someone who had no sense. Quickly, the girlfriend went back to Adam and wrapped herself around him, her hands gently pulling at his face so she could kiss him. "She's an imbecile. You got me, honey. You don't need anyone else."

Adam, losing interest in Mandy, lifted his girl so her legs curled around his waist and he turned away, bored with the theatrics. "Yeah, baby. I got you."

Sam looked disgusted. "Hey, lover-boy, did you collect the stuff I told you to?"

"Yeah, man. It's on the counter over there." Adam nodded his head to where a stack of wallets and cell phones were gathered. Then he went back to feeling up his partner and kissing her neck.

Sam pushed against his back, his stance argumentative and bossy. "Jesus, Adam. Cut that shit out. I told you if you came along there'd be no funny business, and I meant it. Either shape up, or next time stay home and lose out on getting your cut."

Disgruntled, Adam shoved the girl away and pouted. "So, what the fuck do you want me to do now?"

"I want you to have that bitch you shot, her daughter and the rest of the women ready to go out the front door. We're getting the air conditioning turned back on and I need some smokes. You want I should order anything for you and Paul?"

"Yeah. Get some pizza and cans of Red Bull." Adam pulled a mickey out of his back pocket. "I'm starved and thirsty. While you're at it, find out where the hell Michael and John are. You called them at noon and it's after two now."

Chapter Eight

Kandi watched each time as Sam, frustrated and growing more agitated, tried calling Michael, his older brother. He hadn't been able to reach him and neither had the officers they'd put on his trail. Both Michael and John seemed to have disappeared without a trace.

An APB on both their vehicles had turned up nothing. Neither had the agents who'd gone undercover and swept the places the brothers most often hung out. It would be strange enough having one of them disappear, but both at the same time couldn't be a coincidence. The brothers had to be together. But what the hell were they up to? Not knowing was making everyone nervous as hell, including the criminals.

Finally, the pizzas arrived with the drinks, and Kandi called to make the arrangements.

"Hey babe, thanks for the cool air."

"You're welcome, Sam. We made a deal and I always keep my end of the bargain."

"You got our food?"

"Yep. It's hot and ready to be delivered."

"I want you to bring it in."

Dan pulled off his earphones and slammed his hand on the off button, cutting the connection. Everyone swung his way with astonished expressions. The color of his ferocious eyes matched his surname. "Not gonna happen! You get that prick to allow a couple of the male agents to deliver or the deal's off. No compromises. I mean it!"

Kandi bristled and wasn't quite sure how to handle the unusual feeling. Having no doubt her mouth gaped open from the shock of his vehemence, she stuttered her opposition. "Sir, he asked for me." Knowing she'd won Sam's confidence gave them an upper hand. Breaking that link could be disastrous.

Dan's expression didn't change. "Sweet-talk him around. Tell him you don't make deliveries. I don't really care what the fuck you tell him. You're not going into that nest of vipers, and that's it."

Most times in her negotiations, she gave the orders and having Agent Black step on her toes sure didn't sit well, but he was her superior.

Swallowing her uneasiness, she smiled soothingly and agreed. "Fine."

The phone rang, and she straightened her spine, swiped her curls to the back of her head so the earphones fit properly, and pushed the on switch. "I'm sorry, Sam. We got cut off."

"You bringing our stuff over?"

"Sorry, sugar. No can do. I'll send a couple of the agents, and I promise they'll be unarmed."

"No deal. I want you, or no one."

Dan broke in. "Agent Sugar is not cleared to risk her safety in this way. I'll make the delivery."

"Who the fuck do you think you are?"

"I'm the Special Agent in Charge and what I say goes. You want the food and cigarettes; I'll deliver them, or no one will."

On the screen, they watched as Sam bashed the receiver against his free hand. Pissed off would be a mild term for his reaction to Dan's ultimatum. Reaching into his empty pocket seemed to infuriate him even more. No doubt the loss of his smokes helped to sway his decision.

"Whatever. Bring the shit now."

"Are the women ready to come out?"

"Yeah. We have them at the front door. Just stand back until they're free and then you can bring the food in and drop it on the closest counter. And, buddy, you better not be armed, or my trigger-happy brother will plug you and get a kick out of doing so."

Kandi swung to face her new boss. Keeping her voice low, she muttered, "You didn't say you'd be the one to deliver."

"Me or one of the other men. Makes no difference. At least we know Adam isn't going to melt at the sight of my sweet ass." He threw the earphones on the table and glared at her. "*Shit!*" Then he stomped out.

Kandi's eyes grew large and she couldn't help the smile that first appeared on her face before it was quickly wiped off when he cussed. *Holy moly, the boss thinks I have a sweet ass. Or maybe that's not what he meant. Probably he was referring to any woman's ass.* The heat in her face swept throughout her body and she had no doubt even her toes were blushing. Noisy throat-clearing made her turn around to catch the grins on the faces of her colleagues.

Bobbi winked, and Wes linked his fingers under his chin, turned his head at an angle and fluttered his eyelashes.

Kandi laughed.

Chapter Nine

Dan wished his own long legs could reach his butt and give it a good ass-kicking. What the fuck was wrong with him? That woman was going to turn him into a love-sick wuss before he'd finished this job and he'd never be the same. No more love-'em-for-the-night and then walking away satisfied but alone. No more taking pleasure in his lonely lifestyle, his independence and lack of anything even close to a relationship.

Shit! Shit! Shit!

Striding toward the closed-off zone in front of the bank, he rubbed the hair on the back of his neck and dug his fingers in until he felt the pain. *Last time he'd allowed himself to check up on her, she was a desk girl. Why the hell did they switch her to this department? Ethics be damned! He should have investigated before leaving Washington.*

He approached the officers waiting with the food, removed his weapon and handed it to the captain who himself carried a Colt AR-15 M4. Then he did a quick surveillance of the surrounding area. They had everything set up; snipers on the rooftops, ambulances waiting beyond the perimeter and plenty of SWAT members anticipating orders.

Some of the team had wanted to break in, end the holdup and save the hostages, but no one could guarantee they'd be safe. After all, they already had one dead and another wounded. These assholes were lowlifes without any kind of a future. Besides their numerous other charges like robbery, assault and kidnapping, they now faced first degree murder.

Picking up the packages, he moved forward into the open area, hating all the eyes watching as he walked toward a possible death. It had been some time since he'd been in the field and felt the racing adrenalin of facing the unknown. Energy pumped throughout his system and he realized he'd missed the addictive rush.

As soon as he stepped up onto the sidewalk, the bank's door opened and a flurry of women began to appear. Two of the larger ones were trying to support Melissa, while sixteen-year-old Mandy carried Melissa's limp daughter.

Officers, who'd been waiting at the side of the building, appeared, scooped up the lot of them and forced them to safety. Dan, waiting for the entrance to clear, now had an opening and he slowly entered. The slamming of the door behind him was somewhat alarming, and so was the gun he felt digging into his neck.

"Move forward and put the stuff on the counter. Hands in the air, asshole. And keep them there." The hoarse voice could belong to none other than his host, Samuel Dixon.

Dan did as he was told. "Here's what we promised: pizzas, smokes and cold drinks." The smell from the cooked pepperoni and cheese began to permeate the air, and Dan hoped it would soothe the savage beast now pushing him further into the room. "Anything else we can get for you? We want to keep you boys calm and willing to discuss your future choices."

Sam plunged the gun into Dan's shoulder and he knew the bruise would take some time to heal — the bastard. "Hey, the deal was for me to deliver. I brought what you ordered."

"Yeah, well, your deals mean squat to me." Again, the gun left its mark as Sam forced Dan further into the empty space. "Get over there with the rest of the patsies and keep your mouth shut. Anyone pisses me off, and I shoot you first, got it?"

Sam gave Dan a shove and waited until he'd settled next to the man who held a young boy.

"Least you could do is trade the kid for me. He doesn't belong in here, Sam. Let him go, and I'll promise to behave."

Sam laughed just as Dan had hoped he would. "You know what, you're a funny guy. I got me a kid and an FBI bigshot. I've just guaranteed our freedom."

Just then, he turned, catching Paul pulling off a strip of pizza. "Stop, Paul. What if they've added something to the food? Give that bitch the first bite and wait and see if she gets sick or falls asleep. I don't trust those peckers to keep their word."

Dan answered, pushing his luck. "Guess we shouldn't have trusted you to keep yours. Thought the deal was for you to release *all* the women?" Dan could see the glazed eyes of the lone female hostage and pity swelled inside him at her situation.

The grey suit she wore might have looked nice before the bank had been invaded by freaks with low IQs and a penchant for danger. But now, with her blouse hanging out from her skirt and its tie no longer in a jaunty bow but straggling in front, it all looked tacky. Her red, frizzy hair stuck out every which way, the makeup she'd probably applied perfectly before leaving her bathroom this morning now looked like a horror show, and the entreaty in her eyes all but broke his heart—poor, frightened soul.

Paul stepped up to her and shoved the piece of pizza forward, pushing it closer so she had no choice but to take a bite. Crying softly, she tried to chew but gagged and held her hand to her mouth so the food wouldn't fall out. "She's my partner, cop. So, shut the fuck up. She's the keeper of the keys. I need her. We still have a few more boxes to break open. Then, for all I care, Adam can have her." He giggled as if his joke was hilarious, and even Sam broke into a grin. The terrified woman let out a cry, crumpled to the floor and, hugging herself, she began to sway from side to side.

"Give the kid a piece too. See if anything affects him. He's small and it wouldn't take as long." Dan made the hint as if to help them, but in actual fact, he could see the boy's hunger. Only made sense after the hours he'd been penned up.

While he spoke, the couple in the corner caught his eye. The girlfriend, her mouth swollen and cheeks reddened from Adam's roughness, pushed away from the hands that had been all over her and let out a squeal of outrage as Adam snatched at her groin to bring her back to where he wanted her. "I'm hungry, honey." She grovelled prettily. "Let's get something to eat. Can't you smell the pizza?"

Frustration appearing on his flushed face, Adam stopped her escape. Callously hauling her around to face him, he ground out disgusting words everyone could hear. "You've been leading me on all day, bitch. I don't like playing games, so either you spread those long legs of yours or I'm gonna take what you've been dangling in front of me, and the hell with pleasing you."

Swiftly, Sam stomped over to Adam, pushed the girl aside and got into his space. "Shut up, you little prick. Haven't I been telling you this isn't the time or the place? Unlike you, Lexi's just following orders, and if you don't stop hounding the poor girl to death, and pissing me off, I'm gonna throw you out the door and let the cops deal with you."

Swiftly changing his attitude and his stance, Adam's body loosened, and his ingratiating grin would have been slapped off if Dan had his way. "Sorry, bro. My bad." His insincere ass-kissing seemed to work on his big brother who slung his arm around Adam's shoulders.

"Come and get some food. Then start taking these folks to the toilet one by one. Keep the door open and make sure they don't mess around. Okay?"

"Why?" Adam frowned at Sam, his stunned look almost comical.

"Because, it's beginning to smell like an outhouse in here." Sam pulled out a cigarette and lit it and then glared at Adam. "Just do what the fuck I say, okay?"

His mouth full of pizza, Adam nodded. "Yeah, man." Then he grabbed a can of the energy drink, guzzled some liquor from the bottle of alcohol he pulled from his back pocket and washed it down with the other. All the brothers seemed to have stashed alcohol somewhere on their person and pretty soon, they were all mixing drinks and filling their faces.

Dan took the moment to check out Adam's girl, whose name, Lexi, rang a bell. While she stood to the side and daintily chewed her food, he carefully searched her features. Recognition slammed into him like he'd run into a closed window.

Hoping no one but the camera had picked up on his astonishment, he lowered his face until he knew the shock had disappeared and then checked her out again. This time she caught his eye. As he watched, the hint of a wink appeared and faded as quickly.

It was enough.

Chapter Ten

Wes spoke first. "How did the son-of-a-bitch know they weren't going to keep their word?"

"Same way we knew, Wes. Come on... How many times has Cupcake here gone into a situation like this one and been held? More times than not, right?"

Wes turned to Kandi. "Did you suspect?"

"Oh, sure. Actually, I depended on it. The right person could defuse the situation a lot easier on the inside than from here."

"I'm not sure you could have this time, Kandicane." Bobbi wore a serious expression. "At least, the boss didn't. I'm beginning to think he called it right. Those guys are definitely high-maintenance. It might come to a real shoot-out this time."

"Good Lord, I hope not." Kandi continued to

watch the screen and let out an exclamation when she saw the wink that Adam's girlfriend shared with Dan. "Wes, roll it back to where Sam gets Adam to join them at the front of the bank." She pointed at the image on the monitor and then said excitedly, "Slow it down here. Did you hear that? Her name is Lexi. Check it out with missing persons, wanted lists and... you know what? Something tells me you should also go back over the last bunch of charges we had against those boys and see if the name Lexi or Alexi comes up."

"Will do. You think she's been running with them for a while?"

"Nope. But something about her name is nagging at me."

Kandi took over the controls and started the replay again. "Now keep watching carefully when Dan catches her eye."

The silence could be cut with a knife until Bobbi let out an excited snort and Wes swore.

"She winked."

"Oh, yes, she did." Kandi felt a rush of gladness throughout her body. Maybe Dan wasn't all alone in there with those animals after all. Just maybe, he had a friend.

The ringing phone broke the silence. Composing her face, Kandi reached for it and answered softly. "Hello Sam. How's the pizza?"

"Hi, sugar. It's damn good. Best pizza I ever had."

"I'm glad. There seems to be a bit of a problem

though. You also kept our delivery boy."

"Maybe, but I kept the deal we made. You said I had to send out all the women and I did."

"No, Sam, you didn't. Grace Keen, a staff member, is still missing."

"Oh, yeah, about her. She's helping us solve a bit of a mystery in here and as soon as she's finished, to show you I keep my word, I'll send her out too."

"And the delivery guy?" Kandi heard background noises and knew he'd put on the speaker phone: the rustling of clothes and the click of a lighter let her know he'd taken out a cigarette and lit it.

"He's not a female. Besides, you never said I couldn't keep him, Kandi, now did you?"

"Oh, you are a devil, Sam." Kandi chuckled as if she found him amusing. "You remind me of my father."

"You got a dad?"

"Uh? Don't we all?" Teasingly, she lowered her voice to a non-confrontational sound, like one pal joking with another.

He laughed, just as she'd intended. "Sorry, that was a dumb question."

"Hey, it was a dumb answer too. Let me see. My dad. What can I tell you? He's my best friend and my biggest nightmare."

"How so?"

Bobbi came close and watched with Kandi as Sam, relaxed with his cigarette, watched his brother and girlfriend force one victim at a time toward the back of the bank where the bathrooms were located. Leaning toward the phone, he replaced the cigarette package in his pocket but left the receiver on the counter so he could hold onto his gun.

Laughter obvious, she continued talking. "He's a Buddhist... and an inventor. As soon as he finishes one toy, he's on to the next. Lives in a retreat in the mountains and insists I have to stay and look after the family home he built that's full of all his inventions. I love him dearly, but having a father visit whenever the urge takes him and wandering around more often than not in a long, toga-styled robe can be hard to explain."

Laughter in his voice, Sam answered. "You're lucky. My rotten old man's in jail for murder. Guess it runs in the family. Seems like my brothers cloned him, got his genes. I'm peace-loving myself. Like my ma. She was a special lady." Tenderness rang clearly through the line and Kandi felt her heart melt a little.

"She sounds special, Sam. My mom died when I was born so I never knew her. But the ladies at the commune helped bring me up. I guess I was lucky."

Suddenly, Sam straightened, and the look of horror on his face came across clearly on the screen. "Sorry, sugar. I gotta go."

The line went dead, and they watched as Sam rushed to the back. Kandi zeroed in on Dan's face and her heart froze. Anger blazed from his eyes and though she couldn't hear his words, she could clearly make out the F word being used more than once. The only reason Dan stayed in place was that Paul's gun was aimed directly his way and he looked prepared to shoot.

Chapter Eleven

Bobbi spoke first. "What the hell just happened?"

Before anyone could answer, Deputy Harvey knocked and entered. "The Sheriff wants to let you know that they've had a sighting of John, one of the other Dixon boys. There've been a slew of vehicles stolen, all identical black ford vans, with darkened windows and licensed in the same year. One of the officers got lucky with a clip from the car lot video and it shows John clearly as a culprit."

"Thanks Harvey. Can you send me the footage? How many vans are we talking about?"

"After John stole his, one of our staff noticed that the next three calls were about thefts of the same make and color which could mean four so far." He scratched his mustache and then smoothed it down in the habitual way many men did. "Hell if I know why your perps are being so picky, but something tells me we're going to find out."

Before Harvey got started, Kandi gently cut him off with a smile. "Okay, let me know if you get anything else, Harv. And thank the Sheriff for us. This situation is a dynamite keg waiting to explode. We're hoping to keep the lid on it, but I have the feeling something's gonna give soon."

Bobbi interrupted. "Kandi, you need to pay attention to this now. Sam's frothing, Dan looks like he could kill, and Adam's chick has taken a beating."

Kandi quickly put her attention back to the screen and saw what Bobbi meant. Lexi's face looked like it had been punched numerous times, her eye was swollen and her mouth cut. Strangely enough, she'd forced the boy, Kevin, behind her. His arms were wrapped around her waist and she was protecting him with her body.

"Sam, please tell Adam that the kid didn't mean to piss on him. Adam scared him, is all." While Lexi talked, she slowly maneuvered herself and the boy to the side where the hostages were sitting on the floor, until he was close to his father, who, now kneeling with his arms opened beseechingly, sat closest to Dan. They watched as she gave the boy a shove so he ended up safe in his dad's arms.

Before being gathered close, the agents saw

young Kevin also sported a cut lip and tears flooded his white cheeks. Bravely, he flung himself to Daddy and made himself as small as possible while he hid in his father's arms. Daddy looked fit to kill, and only Dan's clutching hand stopped him from rising and becoming confrontational.

"Adam, you stupid bastard!" Sam's yell could be heard all the way outside. "Are you crazy, man? Why'd you want to go and hit the kid? And Lexi? For Chrissakes, you're really beginning to piss me off."

Adam's hand moved fast. His gun appeared from the holster under his arm and ended up in his hand, a move as slick as one saw in the movies. He waved it at the kid and then at Sam. A threat almost... not quite... being delivered. Then he lowered it. "Yeah, well, speaking of getting pissed, that rotten little brat *pissed* on me. Look at my jeans."

Sure enough, there was a small wet stain on his left leg from his knee to the ankle. "Stupid brat said he couldn't go, the crying, snivelling puppy. I got sick of waiting."

Lexi crossed her arms and moved closer to Sam. "Just as Kevin started, Adam swung him around and the boy didn't have time to stop. It was an accident."

"So how come you got the beating?"

"Adam just lost his temper. No biggie. Right, darlin'?" She began to move back to Adam's side, and seemed relieved when he re-holstered his gun, lifted his arm and wrapped it around her neck.

"I got my ol' man's temper. Shouldn'ta hit you, baby. But you keep that little bastard away from me, and we'll be good." Adam's sly, trying-to-look-sexy grin revealed absolutely no remorse.

Sam's disgust showed plainly. "You know what, let's get back to work. Lexi, take these last two assholes for a break, all except the cop. Adam, stay in here and watch everyone closely, make sure they don't do anything stupid. Paul, get Miss Bank-lady there and go back in the vault, hit those last few boxes. I just got a text from Michael and they're on the way. We need to be ready."

Chapter Twelve

"Kandi?"

"Hi, Sam. You had some excitement, heard you yelling all the way outside."

"Yeah. My little brother needs an ass-kicking, didn't get enough when he was younger. Me 'n' my brothers had the ol' man around, and he took good care of seeing that we didn't get too big for our britches. That youngster, Adam, he's just meaner than a hound dog with her tit caught in a trap."

"Ouch! He must be hard to handle."

"Tell me about it. Look, sugar, we're making plans to hightail it outta here. But me 'n' the boys need a favor."

"Sure, what can we do for you?"

"I need you to promise that when my brothers

arrive, you'll un-barricade the street from the west, leave it open so they can get through."

"And if I do that for you?"

"Ah! We're dealing again, huh?"

"It's the way the game is played, Sam. We both know it."

"I'll let the Bank-lady go."

"You already promised to let *her* go. I'm keeping you to your word." Kandi sighed loudly, making sure he could hear her. "I want all the hostages, and then we'll do as you say."

He laughed, softness invaded his tone. It seemed he enjoyed their byplay. "Oh, sugar, darlin', that's *so* not gonna happen. We both know that without these folks, we'd be sitting ducks and wouldn't get a half mile up the road. Tell you what I'll do. How about I let a couple of the men go, the two old bastards that can't hold their bladders. Stinkin' the place up to high heaven. I'll be glad to be rid of the old dudes."

"I want all the men, the father with his kid too."

"Not gonna happen, honey. Unless..."

Kandi heard Bobbi's voice behind her. "Shit! Don't do it, Kandi."

Kandi waved her quiet and answered. "Unless..."

"If you join us, I'll give up all the men."

"Liar."

"Hey, you're hurting my feelings."

"Then don't lie to me. Give me everyone and I'll

come in. At least you know you can rely on my word."

"Kandi baby, I gotta say, I like you. And it hurts me like hell to refuse to give you what you want."

"Okay then, keep Agent Black, I'll come in and you let the civilians go. If you have two federal agents as hostages, no one will stand in your way. And, Sam, sugar...that's the very best I can do." This time her voice firmed, sending out conciliatory vibes that were also resolute.

He hesitated. "Hold on a minute, honey." They watched him lower the phone to the counter, pull his cigarettes from his pocket and light one. The man's craggy face, with a two-day beard and large eyes, looked toward the camera as if he knew it existed.

For the first time, she got a really good look at his features. His face had a lived-in kind of appearance, along with a few pock marks that only added to the over-all look of a strangely handsome man. He could be someone she might meet in a... a bar. Nah, she never went to bars—didn't know how to handle the drunks without them confiding in her about their sad lives by the end of the night.

Bobbi moved in front of her. She wanted Kandi to watch as she moved the side of her hand across her throat in a clear message that meant, *cut this off now.*

Kandi shook her head, waiting and watching.

Wes rolled his chair closer. "The boss'll be

pissed, cupcake. You sure you know what you're doing?"

First, she caught Bobbi's eye, and then Wes's. "All I'm doing is my job. Get as many hostages to safety as possible. If in the last resort, you can negotiate to replace someone in danger, then use your own judgement. That's what I'm doing."

"The asshole lied before, when Dan went in. Kept back Grace Keen. What's to say he won't do it again?"

"I won't go into the building until they're all safely—"

Bobbi interrupted, "Yeah, well, good luck with that." Bobbi straightened her shoulders. "I'm going in as you. They have no idea what you look like. They won't make me until it's too late."

"And as soon as you open your mouth, he'll shoot you just for pissing him off." Wes didn't pull his punches.

Suddenly, Sam picked up the phone. Kandi could see Dan in the background. He'd been listening to Sam's side of the conversation. The slight negative move of his head and the fierce look on his face came across loud and clear.

She ignored his signal. "Have you decided, Sam? Do we have a deal?"

"You'll let my brothers through? There're two vans."

Two? Whaa?

"Two vans? Fine. I'll give the stand-down order.

What's their estimated time of arrival?"

"Should be here in ten minutes; as soon as I give them the all-clear."

"And you'll have the hostages ready to come out when I appear?"

"Yep. And honey, I checked you up on Google, so I know what you look like. Don't try any foolish moves."

"Would I do that to you?" She made sure her voice softened again. "I never lie, Sam. I give my word: I stick to it. Can I trust you to do the same?"

His split-second hesitation rang out clearly, and Bobbi viciously pointed to the grinning figure on the monitor.

"Of course, you can. We'll start rounding up the gang and be waiting to welcome you to our happy little party."

Chapter Thirteen

When Sam ended the call, Dan couldn't believe his ears. That maddening, curly-headed, big-hearted, dizzy chick had negotiated to take someone's place against his specific orders. *Blasted obstinate female!*

Unconsciously, he reached into his pocket and realized he'd left his wallet back at the mobile center. A picture he'd carried around with him for years rested in the back slot. He'd ripped out the photo from a school yearbook of a girl around eleven years old, taken when he would have just turned fourteen.

The well-worn picture had given him much-needed comfort when life had gotten too dark. When it wasn't accessible, he'd close his eyes and picture the sweet angel sitting at her regular seat on the bus. With her golden hair a cloud of sunlight around her face, every morning, she'd smiled just for him.

The first time he'd seen her, his foolish adoring heart had lifted out of his chest. And if the truth were told, he'd have to admit that it had never been returned.

That morning he'd taken a particularly bad beating from a foster father, who shouldn't have been in charge of a kid, and he'd decided to run away. The chance of meeting her on the same bus the next day had stopped him. He'd traveled on that bus for most of the year and had talked to her only once. Just knowing she was safe and still smiling had been enough for the desperately shy, insecure boy he'd been.

Shaking himself from dwelling in the past, he clenched his hands and fought off the chills that attacked his body. Agent Kandice Warner's beautiful smile reminded him of that young girl. So did the sparkles in her shining eyes.

Goddammit, being watched like some animal in a cage, he couldn't make a move without Sam swinging his gun in his direction. With the boy so close... shit!

At the very least, he hoped Kandice would be smart enough to wear a tracking device. Since it looks like they'd be travelling, he wanted to know the SWAT team would be hot on their trail.

Grinding his teeth, he looked around at the other seven victims who were still confined with him. Two older men, sitting in a stinking pool from bladder problems, looked all in, as if they'd given up hope. Perched against the nearby wall, their heads drooping, pants stained and hopeless eyes bloodshot and bleary, they pulled at his conscience. It was his job to protect them...

The father and boy next to him were the ones he knew were in grave danger. If he had control of who stayed and who left, he'd give up both of the gramps without a qualm before he'd release the kid. There wasn't a cop on the force or a Fed on the books who'd take any unnecessary chances with the boy around, and that bastard Sam knew it. What he didn't know was those same men and women would give up their lives to save a child too.

Glancing to his right, two other men, both of whom had kept a low profile, seemed accepting but constantly watchful. The heavier of the two, an obvious hands-on guy, maybe a carpenter from the look of his clothes, nodded when he saw Dan checking him out. Dan returned the gesture and hoped if anything went down, he could rely on this dude to keep his head.

The other male, a businessman whose attire suggested a rather prominent and successful career, had already tried bribing his way out. The dumb ass sported a bruise from the kick Sam had given him as a response to his plea for special treatment. Wallowing, he sat with his head in his hands sniffling. *Asshole!*

Dan knew he mustn't forget poor Grace, who was working in the vault again with Paul. At least Paul had treated her half decently. As far as Dan could tell, other than the horrifying stress of being in constant danger, Paul hadn't laid a finger on her. He'd forced her to open the hundreds of safety deposit boxes but without getting violent or physical. Not that he didn't have it in him... after all, he was a Dixon.

That left only himself and Lexi. Since she'd taken the beating for the boy, Dan had moved her onto the victims' list and observed as she played Adam. Watching closely, he could see her frustration with the idiot. Go figure. He was the only one of the gang who used a fancy leather holster for his weapon, like some new-age narc. He wore it close to his body, under his right arm, and it was quite the contraption.

Snuggled tightly, the gun, a long-barrelled Glock 20, was deadly and likely held fifteen rounds, more power than anyone needed for an everyday firearm. Was she trying to take it off him? Or get him to lay it down? Dan wished he knew what her game was.

Straining to hear, he listened in on their conversation. "Adam, honey, let's go into the back. I don't fancy screwing in front of the folks when we can be alone, take our clothes off and enjoy ourselves, do you?"

Dan heard Adam groan and then in a rough

voice he answered, "Can't now, baby. Sam's already pissed at me. We gotta go help Paul pack the stuff. My other brothers'll be here shortly to get us. Once we're safely at the place, I promise we'll have the whole night together."

The place? Must be a hideout they recently found. Before coming in, Dan'd scanned all the data they had on the brothers and he hadn't found any mention of a home base.

From what he could tell, they moved around a lot and had recently arrived from Chicago. One thing he'd give them; they stayed together, worked as a family, and big brother Michael kept tight control. Which made Dan wonder why Sam and the boys had played outside the lines on this job. Were they trying to show off for Michael? Or had this scenario with the family been planned all along?

Glad now that the idiots hadn't searched him well when he'd arrived, Dan felt better for having the knife he'd hidden in his boot. There'd been a few times he'd had to use it in his career, and today, at the last minute, he'd fetched the boots from his vehicle and inserted it in the hidden slot he'd had fabricated.

Feeling sure that before the night was over he'd be glad to have it, he concentrated on loosening the tense muscles that had formed after Sam's last phone call.

Suddenly, Sam came closer. He pointed at the

old guys and barked out an order. "You two, get up and come with me. Looks like it's your lucky night, thanks to Agent Warner."

"Can I leave now? I promise not to tell them anything if you let me go. I don't know anything; I just need to get out of here." The sad-assed businessman sniveled his plea and half rose.

Dan grabbed at his jacket and hauled him back down before the kick aimed his way connected to his head. "Sam, you don't want to injure a hostage. Think about it. It's better to keep us healthy and moving on our own, right?"

Sam's frustrated growl let Dan know he didn't want to listen, but knew Dan's comment had made good sense. Dan half-turned away but something made him pivot back in time to see Sam backhand the weasel who hadn't seemed able to accept good advice. The stupid prick had struggled away from Dan and started to get up again. Now he lay prone, having landed on the carpenter, who'd sneered before pushing him aside.

Registering Sam's expression of pleasure, Dan guessed he liked hitting folks. "Hey, man, if you let the boy out, it would go a long way in your favor, especially with... ah, Agent Warner. She loves kids."

Sam stared at him, his hard eyes glittering. Dan watched the evil grin fade, leaving a well-used *who-gives-a-shit* expression. Strangely, this time it didn't ring true.

The commotion outside caught everyone's attention. Quickly, Sam rounded up the men, other than Dan, and forced them to stand on the left side of the door.

Having been trained to pay attention to even the smallest detail, Dan remembered that the door opened to that side, and he knew those folks would be behind the open door. That meant that Sam would wait for Kandi to enter before he'd let anyone leave.

When he saw how Sam had forced the two oldest at the front of the line and the father and son at the end of it, he caught on. Hatred roared through his veins, reminding him of the only hit of speed he'd ever taken as a stupid kid.

Before he could comment, Paul had forced Grace out of the vault. Dragging two heavy sacks, he loped into the room and set his precious cargo down with a thump on the grey and white speckled granite floor. "Hey, Sam, you were right." He waved a purple satin bag. "We finally hit the box, but it wasn't thirty-two. It was three hundred and thirty-three. You need to get your ears checked, man."

Adam, followed by Lexi, carried another two satchels filled with valuables, and interrupted Sam cuffing Paul teasingly. "Hey, watch the hostages, man. Dopey's trying to escape."

Sure enough, the businessman had seen his moment and decided to take a chance on getting away. Only the lock on the door wouldn't turn easily and as he was shaking so badly, he hadn't been able to open it.

Before Sam could take aim, Dan rolled over and dragged the jackass to the floor and shoved him behind his body. "No more bloodshed, Sam. Not smart."

Glaring his disgust, Sam stomped right up to him. Without taking his cruel eyes off Dan, he snarled, "Get back in line, you sorry-son-of-a-bitch." Suddenly he turned on the scurrying body and kicked his ass hard. "You mess up one more time, man, and I'm gonna shoot you right between your shifty eyes, got it?" With his gun aimed at the very target, no one with half a brain would question if he meant business.

Before the other could stop blubbering long enough to answer, two things happened simultaneously. The phone rang. And two black vans pulled up in front of the building about three feet from the front door.

Showtime!

Chapter Fourteen

Kandi had changed into her SWAT outfit of tight black pants, long-sleeved white t-shirt and Kevlar vest. She hooked her badge to the belt around her waist and hoped that the tracking device installed in the belt buckle didn't get spotted.

She tucked the lipstick tube her father had made for her into the side pocket of her tight pants and patted it in place.

Lastly, she slipped her feet into comfortable boots that were a hell of a lot more sensible than the high-heeled suckers she wore most days. A comb through her hair, the application of some lipstick, and she felt ready to face whatever the karmic spirits had in store.

Seeing Dan Black as a hostage had added

another level of fear to an already frightening situation. Why he mattered to such a degree, she didn't know. But he did. At least that's what the ache in her heart signified. Seeing him as a hostage had made her mouth go dry, her body tighten and prayers flood her mind. *Keep him safe. Please God!*

His dark eyes had shot warnings she'd ignored. Didn't mean the warnings hadn't mattered. Because of his rank, because he was her superior, of course his orders mattered. But she couldn't obey him. Not only did the hostages need her on their side, but her needs counted too. And she needed to do everything in her power to save that ornery man.

Bobbi approached and warned her. "That Sam might have a smooth way of talking, cookie, but the bastard's got a quick temper. You watch him, he's one mean prick."

"I pretty well figured that out on my own. But no one is all bad, Bobbi. He told me his dad beat him with a belt when he was a boy, and that could turn anyone nasty. And that he loves his mom. You can tell he cares about his brothers. There's goodness in everyone."

"No, Kandi, not everyone. A psychopath has no heart, no conscience and couldn't give a good Goddamn if he hurts another person. Don't you forget it! You've wanted to learn how to take care of yourself, my friend; Wes and I are worried this just might be the real start to your curriculum."

Bobbi wrapped her arms around her and hung on. "Have you got your lipstick?"

"Of course."

"Okay, good. Cupcake, please don't get hurt. We need you around here. You keep us human."

Wes waited outside the van and sprang forward as soon as he spotted Kandi. "You're set to go. I got the tracking device connected. Still think you should wear a wire, Kandi. They might not search you very well, they didn't with Dan."

"Can't take the chance, Wes. Big brother Michael will be there now, and we both know he's far from stupid." Sharing a quick hug, she pushed away and wiped her hands on the legs of her pants. "I'm ready."

"Got your lipstick?"

"Yep!"

Before they moved another step, two vans drove up to the front of the bank and honked their horns.

"Bye, guys. See you later." She strode forward into the dark, passed the Sheriff and the other SWAT members with a smile at their thumbs-up signals, and then she stood in the light from the bank's doorway. Every man there stood at alert, ready. The snipers were in place, holding, in case they had a shot.

From where she waited, she made out the lineup of the hostages. Grace Keen, looking as if she'd collapse any minute, stood trembling at the very front, followed by two older men, then two younger guys and last in the line was the father carrying his son.

Oh, that's not good! The bastard was trying to play her for a fool. Those vans could hold up to seven people if they were strapped in, and a lot more if they just forced them onto the floors. If Sam stuck to the agreement, there were five brothers and her and Dan. But she knew that wouldn't happen. If he kept the father and son too, there'd be nine; four in one van and five in another... totally doable.

Thinking quickly, she prayed Sam would keep at least a part of his bargain and some of those poor folks would be free in a short time. She watched through the window and saw Dan on the floor next to a plant on the other side of the door. Adam had his gun aimed at Dan's head, while Lexi stood near him with one of the smaller bundles swung over her shoulder.

Two big sacks had also been dragged forward and were sitting near the front door, waiting to be transported to the vans. Sam spoke and pointed, and the two younger men, the carpenter and businessman, stepped out of line and each picked up a satchel. Then he and Paul grabbed a satchel each and they stood waiting.

The sliding van doors opened on the bank side of each vehicle and Kandi sensed guns pointing at her back.

Time to play the game...

Chapter Fifteen

Everything seemed to happen at once. Later, when Kandi watched the sequence of events that the camera had recorded from inside the bank, it made a lot more sense. But at the time, it was pure pandemonium.

Sam had made Grace pull the one bank door open, and he gestured for her to move back inside in order to let Kandi step through.

Though every instinct Kandice possessed urged her to get the hell out of there, she stepped past Grace with an encouraging smile and a pat on her arm.

"Hello, sugar." Sam closed in on her. Empty, dark brown eyes studied her, and a light started to appear deep within them, followed by a sweet smile that shocked Kandi to the very depths of her soul. An impatient honk broke up the moment.

Kandi spoke, "Hiya, Sam. I'm glad to see you're holding up your end of the bargain."

"I'm sorry, baby. I wanted to, but no can do. We'll take them all with us."

At that moment, hearing she'd most likely be still held as a prisoner, Grace broke for safety. Screaming, she charged out of the open door, her arms failing, running to where she could see safety in the line of police cars which were closing off the end of the street, from where the vans had driven through. Clearly visible were police officers with guns behind every open door.

***

Lexi, realizing that Adam had turned his back on her to see what had just happened, swung the heavy sack of goodies she carried and let him have it in the back of the head.

Dan, having understood her earlier signal of intending to stop their escape, tripped Adam and, when the prick went down, he grabbed his weapon, drove the handle against Adam's temple to knock him out and yelled at Lexi to get into the vault.

Pandemonium exploded from the converging incidents. Once Dan had made his move, the frightened captives all began pushing at each other. The father shielding his son, Lexi having stopped to guide him, headed for the closest safe place, which was the vault.

The carpenter, busy helping the two old dudes scramble behind the bank's counter, had his hands full, while the businessman crouched down in their way, held his hands over his head and howled.

Not taking any chances on shooting the victims, instead Dan headed toward where Sam had grabbed Kandice, forcing her in front of him.

Meanwhile the cops outside had opened fire on the vans. The first had driven off into the night, while the second waited, and a harsh voice from inside screamed an order to Sam: "Forget the fucking chick, Sam. Get your ass in here now."

Sam whispered something to Kandi and then threw her toward Dan, making him drop his gun to catch her. While the law-breaking asshole dove through the open side of the van, Dan gently swung Kandi aside but didn't see Paul there. She ended up right in his path.

That idiot, not willing to give up what he'd worked for all day, was trying to haul ass and his sacks too, which turned out to be his biggest mistake. When he got close to the door, Kandice tripped up the son-of-a-bitch with a move straight out of training academy, and then she shot a stream of spray into his face with a friggin' tube of lipstick.

Shockingly, the poor dude erupted in screams of agony, dropped to the floor and began writhing while clutching at his face.

When it landed on the hard floor, the bag of

money and jewels burst open, with loot spreading in every direction and making traction impossible.

Before Dan could get clear, Sam had dove into the moving van, which peeled rubber and screeched off into the night. By now, Dan had freed the knife from his boot and, scrambling through the mess on the floor, he tore outside, and with a Herculean effort, he threw it at the back tire when the van slowed to take the corner. Pleased when it made a direct hit, he saw the van swerve almost out of control.

Unfortunately, whoever was driving handled the situation like a pro, because the van righted itself and kept going, police vehicles in hot pursuit.

Wesley, behind the wheel of the Fed's SUV, screeched to a stop to pick up Dan. Bobbi rode shotgun. They followed, but it was soon clear that the robbers had planned their getaway well.

Traffic had blocked the entrance to an alley they'd used to swing back around, and as the department's vehicles headed in one direction following two bogus black identical vans, Sam and his brothers drove the opposite way.

Wes hit the steering wheel hard and looked at Dan in the rear-view, a scowl on his chubby face. "Sneaky bastards."

"How did you know we'd need to give chase?"

"We had a tracer on Kandi in case she got into the van," Bobbi answered. "We'd never have let her move in without one. Plus, we know that chick;

when she's in her role, you never know what to expect."

Dan sat in total frustration as his co-worker handled the SUV cautiously and Bobbi rode his ass. "You drive like an old woman, Wes. I told you to let me take the wheel."

"I didn't want to end up in a hospital tonight, lady. Besides, you've wrecked your quota of cars this year already."

Hunching her shoulders in a pouting way, Bobbi answered sourly, "Sure. You let Kandi drive."

"Yeah, well, she's a cool cat behind the wheel. You're like a tiger gone bonkers, no limits."

"And you're so not funny. Let's get back to the bank."

Chapter Sixteen

Kandice, trying to be everywhere at once, called the officers to escort Paul to the ambulance in handcuffs. The pepper spray her dad had added to the lipstick tube had a short effect, and she wanted Paul safely in custody before it wore off.

She thanked the carpenter and made sure the two elderly men were okay to go under their own steam to get to the ambulances and didn't need stretchers.

Once they headed for the door, she went into the vault and watched as Lexi hugged the little boy close while his father, shaking badly, remained in the doorway clutching a safety deposit box as a supposed weapon.

Now that the danger had disappeared, it seemed

his strength had gone with it. His arms hung weakly by his side and seeing her, a silly grin appeared on his face. Knowing that shock could affect people in all kinds of ways, Kandi smiled and handed him one of the blankets she'd fetched from one of the ER folks. Then she went over to give others to Lexi and the boy.

Making sure the little guy was well wrapped, Lexi kissed his cheek and then carefully passed him to his father. "He's not scared anymore, are you, Kevin?"

Fighting to stay with her, clinging tightly, Kevin hid his face in her neck. His dad rubbed his back and caressed his head. "You've been so brave, son. I was very proud of you today." Only a father could speak with such loving gentleness in a man's deep voice.

Lexi squeezed the small body and then forced him away from her. "I have to go with the officer now, Kevin. I'm so sorry you had to go through such a nightmare, kid, but you have a wonderful dad and he'll look after you and your mom."

Kevin leaned back and looked into her eyes. "I don't have a mom. It's just me 'n Dad."

Lexi glanced at the hovering man and smiled sadly. "He's a brave boy, you're very fortunate."

"It could have been a lot worse if you hadn't stepped in, Lexi."

"Actually, it's Alexia. Alexia Forman. That gang hurt my family some time ago, and I had thought to get my revenge today. I just didn't realize they had plans to rob a bank and kill that poor bank manager." She started to cry, and Kandi gathered her close while Kevin hugged her again. Even the father stepped forward as if to share a group hug, obviously upset by the girl's breakdown.

"We'll get you the best lawyer, Alexia—"

Interrupting, her voice breaking, Alexia added, "I can't afford a good lawyer."

"We can, Alexia, can't we, Kevin? It would be my honor to help you with anything it takes to get you free from the charges against you." The father turned toward the two officers who had waited at the doorway after the signal Kandi had given.

One of the officers spoke, his voice stiff with resentment. "Aggravated assault, murder and kidnapping to start with..."

Kandi watched as Alexia passed the crying boy to his daddy and then walked to the cops and turned, holding her hands behind her back for them to put on the cuffs.

"I understand."

Kandi added, "No. You don't, Alexia. I have a lot of video proving your heroics most likely saved the lives of the hostages and stopped Adam from killing yet another person. I'll be happy to share this with the prosecutor, and I know that it will work in your favor."

Alexia looked at her, a wry grin on her face without any other sign of humor. "Oh, no. I don't think you understand. Adam is bad news, but he didn't kill anyone."

"Then who killed the bank manager?"

Alexia and Kevin's dad answered simultaneously.

"Sam did."

Chapter Seventeen

"I want to know what he said to you." Dan waylaid Kandi after they'd returned to the office, and he wasn't budging from the looks of it. At least, not until she'd satisfied his inquiry.

"Are you talking about Sam?"

"Yes. Before he left, he whispered something and I saw your face freeze with distaste or possibly fear."

"Most likely confusion. All he said was, "Next time." I'm not sure I understood what he meant. Did you know Sam killed the bank manager? Both Alexia Forman and Pat Wagner confirmed it."

"You sound shocked."

"He had me fooled. I thought he had a heart hidden inside him somewhere."

"Kandice, the man's a psychopath. They don't have hearts." Dan's pose changed from relaxed to slightly aggressive; as if he could force-feed her facts so she'd understand what he so obviously understood.

"That's what Bobbi and Wes said too. But I can't believe it. He loved his mother, I know he did."

Dan's hard attitude softened slightly. "Maybe, but he'll always love Sam Dixon more." As if he couldn't help himself, he reached for her hand and she let him hold it although his touch made her tremble. "I saw the way he looked at you."

"What do you mean? He just looked indecisive."

"No. He looked torn. It's totally different. He didn't want to leave you, Kandice. If he could have, he'd have taken you with him in a flash."

"Then why didn't he? He had me by the door. No one would have shot him when he held a federal officer."

"I would have. I had a clear shot. And he knew it."

Kandi stiffened. "Then why didn't you take it?"

"Because he shoved you my way. He knew I wouldn't shoot with you in between."

"Oh! Everything happened so fast, I didn't realize. So, the other three Dixon boys are still on the loose?"

While one fist got a rubdown from the other hand, Dan grunted his yes. "Sneaky bastards stole four vans. We knew it. We'd gotten the license numbers from the ones they drove to the bank, but they switched. The uniforms came across the first two abandoned not long ago."

He looked down at his shoes and then shot her a fierce stare. "Do you live alone, Agent Warner?"

Kandi's face fell. "So, we're back to Agent Warner?"

Thrown for a loop, Dan didn't know quite how to answer. He read her confusion and it dawned on him that she'd follow his lead and he wasn't being very obliging. "Hell, sugar, I'll call you whatever the hell you want me to call you, as long as you promise me you won't stay alone until we catch this guy."

Kandi backed up, his vehemence too much for her to handle in her precarious state of mind. Most incidents she was called on to deal with involved some type of mental issue; either people who wanted to hurt themselves or take another with them. But today's events had tapped her reserves. "Alone, sir? I don't understand. Agent Black—"

"Oh, for Chrissakes, call me Dan." His blasted eye began twitching, or at least the skin under it did, and he rubbed at his cheek to cover it up. When overwhelmed with frustration, the stupid spasms often got the better of him.

Apparently not liking his tone, she glared her displeasure and continued. "Fine, Agent Dan. Yes, I do live alone, but in a huge house loaded with every type of security you can imagine — some the world has never seen, thanks to my dad's innovative inventions. I'm perfectly safe."

He'd read a bit about her circumstances in her personnel file and knew her father was now considered a genius in the methodical scientific community, and not just for his most popular inventions which had garnered him millions. But for clever gadgets he'd never merchandised. Still... Dan didn't like the notion of her being alone. "Do you have a guard dog?"

"Uh...no. So far Dad hasn't come up with that invention yet." She smiled coaxingly, and Dan found himself soothed by her beguiling disposition.

Before she could walk away, he added, "I have a trained dog who will keep you safe. I'll drop him off at your place later. He'll stay outside and guard the perimeter. No one will get past that animal."

She stopped and looked back at him, a smile lighting her features. "Why, is his name Killer?"

Dan had to turn away or give in to her charm. "His name is Blue."

"I get it. Anyone messes with you guys and they end up black and blue." She giggled at her own joke but stopped rather quickly when his stern expression didn't change. "You're a very serious man. It would be better if you could loosen up and relax now that the danger is over, Dan."

"Uh huh, Cupcake. Don't become complacent. Sam is still on the loose. It's not over yet. Not by a long shot. See you later."

Chapter Eighteen

By the time Kandi drove into her winding driveway, she felt completely zapped. Pushing the garage opener which turned on lights throughout the house and its grounds, she waited to make sure the heat sensors were disarmed so they wouldn't set off an alarm when she left the confines of her car.

Her father had set up a new-age system that drove her crazy some days. If anyone were foolish enough to invade her privacy, doors to some of the rooms in the house and garage would automatically lock and refuse to open. Steel netting would suddenly slide out of the enclosures and appear over the windows. And every exit would be impenetrable. In other words, the intruder would be trapped. An alarm call would be automatically sent to the local precinct and to her cell phone, and she would know not to enter because of the danger.

If she happened to already be inside, no one could get at her in certain places where the barricades worked. There were rooms she knew would seal and keep her safe. Problem was, she sometimes forgot, and then all hell would break loose.

Thankfully, once she entered the building and disarmed some of the codes, the house would be just an ordinary residence. But she always carried the remote control with her. Any time she needed to, with the push of a button, she could arm the system and make her house the safest place in the city. So far, other than for her screw-ups, it hadn't been necessary.

Heading to the kitchen, she went to start the tea maker her father had set up with all her favorites in special slots. A push of a button over whichever blend she chose, and the exact amount would drop into the cylinder, where boiling water then poured in and steeped it. Within a few moments, she had the perfect cup of indulgence.

At times like this, when exhaustion reigned, she appreciated her brilliant dad. Often, she wished she could live normally like other working girls her age, in a small apartment downtown that was easy to clean and look after, rather than the mausoleum he insisted she needed. But tonight, she accepted and valued the luxuries.

Grabbing her favorite happy-face mug and a box of decadent chocolate-covered cookies, she headed for her private suite where her dad set her up with not only a bedroom fit for a princess, but a fully-equipped gym, a huge walk-in closet that surprisingly held a modest amount of clothes and an ensuite bathroom to die for.

If the truth were told, her luxurious bubble tub was the one comfort she'd fight to keep. Bathing with a selection of music piped in at the touch of a button, lighting at whatever level she chose, and a crystal fireplace that took up most of one wall nearest the large tub, had to be her idea of paradise.

Heading there now, just as she started up the floating staircase, the doorbell rang followed by a dog's bark. *What in the world?*

She hurried to open the door and met with Dan Black's scowl.

"Did you look through the peephole before opening?"

"What? Why would you ask me that?"

"Because I heard your footsteps, and there was no hesitation before you arrived and the door opened." He glanced over his shoulder at the darkness behind him. "I thought you said you had good security."

She showed him the remote control and mumbled. "I switched it off when I arrived. But

I would have turned it on again before I went to bed."

"You need to leave it on whenever you're home. Can we come in?"

"Oh, of course. Yes. Please." She placed her tea and the box of cookies onto the small ledge by the door and dropped to her knees in front of a large, black, German Shepherd with brown facial markings around his intelligent eyes. "Hi, there, Blue. Aren't you a sweetheart?" She held out her hand and waited for the dog to sniff, to get used to her scent.

The dog ignored her hand and looked toward Dan, waiting for some signal. "No, he's not a sweetheart. He's a guard dog. Okay, Blue."

Once the order was given, the dog approached her slowly, taking his time, and flinching when she caressed his neck. He seemed uncomfortable with her ministrations, so she backed off somewhat and just patted him gently.

She waited until he made eye contact, and she smiled to let the animal know she held no threat. Not liking it, Blue backed away, sat beside Dan and waited for further instructions.

"We need to take him around the perimeter of the house so he knows his territory. Once he's aware of his limitations, he'll patrol the area and won't leave until you call him to be fed."

"I'll get my jacket." As they walked the grounds, Kandi asked, "Can't he stay inside with me? It's cool out here at night. He could protect me from there just as well." She hoped Dan wouldn't be angry with her question, but it made perfect sense to her.

"You'd want him in your house?"

"Of course. I've always wanted a dog, but knew that my long hours away from home wouldn't be fair to the animal. He's a lovely animal... and very gentle." She reached down and ran her hand over the dog's fur. Blue ignored her strokes and continued to walk along, every so often veering away to mark a tree on their rounds.

"Agent..."

Her throat clearing made him change his mind.

"Kandice, Blue is not a pet. He's a working dog who knows the rules. If you treat him differently from what he's used to, he'll become confused. He's here to guard you, nothing more."

"So, you're saying we can't be friends."

He stopped and looked at her, the lights now bright around the building. "Friends? And that's important to you?"

"Very."

Dan seemed baffled and glanced at her feet rather than in her face. With his tone softening, he spoke quietly. "What is it that you want, Kandice?"

Taking his behavior personally, she just had to ask. "I want to know why you don't like me."

Now she got his attention.

"Why would you assume that I don't *like* you?"

His voice had become louder, frustration apparent.

"Because you never look at me when we're talking. It's like you can't stand to see my face."

"Hell, it's not because I don't like you, woman." Dan's tone rose even more, and anger bubbled. Both were surprised when Blue growled low with warning. Rubbing his eye, Dan blinked a few times as if something were wrong. Then he turned to walk away from her, stopped and hesitated. "You remind me of someone I lost. Look, we have to work together. I need to keep things professional. You're all... ah, personal and that's just not my way."

"Then you do like me."

"Oh, for Chrissakes, yes, I like you already. Are you satisfied?" Driven, he'd moved into her space, overpowering her with his height and the full force of his magnetism. "Blue, back off!"

The dog's fur stiffened on his neck and a menacing noise came from his throat, but he stepped away, his eyes never leaving his master.

"How the fuck do you do it? Every man in the place and most of the women adore you. Now you've got the blasted dog under your spell. I'm..." He stopped and drove his fingers through his short, dark hair, rumpling it attractively.

Too shy to encourage him to continue, she'd have given up her best pair of Jimmy Choos for him to finish. He didn't. Instead he stared into her face, his eyes roaming over her features and a sweet side grin he couldn't hold back made her inch forward. She'd never yearned for a man to kiss her before. But at this moment, it was all she craved.

His lips on hers... His hands caressing her body... The two of them joined; her soft heat and his hard danger — a potent combination.

Tension ramped up and she swayed towards him, her eyes begging him. *Kiss me. Oh, please...*

His hands framed her face, pushing her curls aside. He stared as if searching for a person he remembered.

She smiled her approval, her anticipation, and then her adoration. This big, strong, powerful man liked her and her feelings for him were all tied up in knots of wishing and hoping.

Her hand reached up and she cupped his cheek gently, surprised when he closed his eyes and pushed against her palm, nudging against her as if her touch were vital. His eyes closed, and he sighed.

Not being able to stop herself, she nuzzled his face, her lips placing soft kisses everywhere she could reach. When he didn't stop her, she wrapped her arms around his neck and gloried in the sensation of happiness when he hugged her back. Now, splayed against him, her body cuddled close, she leaned back and whispered, "Kiss me."

When his lips touched hers, gently... oh, so gently, she enjoyed the soft caresses but soon she craved more. "Danny, *kiss* me."

Control snapping, breaking apart, he swept her closer and every nerve she owned began to clamor its satisfaction. His lips burned hers like a branding iron of possession. She'd never felt so alive, so vital.

So alone... when he abruptly tore away from her and headed back toward the house. His abrupt words were a shock. "You're tired."

"Oh, God! No, I'm not. I'm wide awake. Not at all tired." Babbling, she followed behind him, talking to his back.

"Yes. You are. And if you aren't, then I am. It's late. The dog is hungry. Fuck, I gotta get out of here before I do something we both know can't happen."

"What? What do you want to do?" Almost out of breath, she tracked him to his car and stopped him from closing the door after he got behind the wheel. "Why can't it happen?"

"Because, this time... God help me. This time, I wouldn't survive."

Chapter Nineteen

Watching the tail lights of his vehicle fade into the distance, heart heavy in her chest, Kandi finally decided Dan wouldn't turn around. "Come on Blue. It's you and me." She waited for the dog to step into the house, and then she set the alarm code and turned off the lights.

Still shaking with reaction, she fetched a big bowl for Blue and filled it with water. Then she carried it to her bedroom where he seemed to find a spot near the door that he liked.

After he was settled, she ran her bath, turned on the fireplace and shut off the rest of the lights. Sinking into the hot water, she turned on the bubbles, a favorite love song... and then she cried like a heartbroken child.

***

After he'd driven like a maniac for a few minutes, Dan forced himself to slow down. Taking his heated dissatisfaction out on his vehicle might result in him hurting others, and that couldn't be allowed. After all, he'd given years of his life to protect the public. And it was all because of her... his precious angel, as he called the girl in the photograph.

Revisiting the past as he often did, he remembered the first time she'd spoken to him. She'd thanked him for protecting her from a bully who took the same bus. The smart-assed kid had decided he'd sit with her, and began to taunt her about the colorful kittens and puppies she'd used as decorations on her binder.

White-blonde hair shimmering from the sunlight through the bus window, face pale and her pretty blue eyes filling, she'd tried to go along with him, to smile at his taunts. But he'd gone way past funny to being hurtful. The little doll had no idea how to handle her tubby tormenter.

But Dan did.

As a thirteen-year-old who'd suffered since he could remember, he'd understood pain and how it could influence people into behaving in a particular way. Using this concept, he'd grabbed the harasser's hand and twisted his wrist back until the kid had slid from his seat to the floor. "Apologize."

It came quickly. "I – I'm sorry. I was kidding."

"It's okay." She'd turned her globby eyes on Dan and her words hit him like bricks on both sides of his head. "Don't hurt him. He's sorry."

Dan understood how cheap those words of apology really were, but seeing the softness and worry that brimmed from her eyes he backed off with a whispered warning to the cringing idiot. He knew from the nod and fear in the other's eyes that it had been taken as seriously as he'd meant it. She wouldn't be bothered again, at least, not by this creep.

Usually she and he were the first passengers on the bus, and from then on, he'd sit in the seat across the aisle from her. As he boarded the bus, she'd always smile her hello. And every day for that whole year, he'd watched over her until...

Now a horn honked behind him, making him shake off the memories, before turning down his new street to the fancy furnished condo he'd booked into while he was in Seattle. It lacked the amenities he had in his small home in Washington—the big patio, pool and the large yard for Blue—but for the time being it suited his purpose.

Once parked, he flipped the light on inside the SUV and removed his wallet. Fingering the photograph hidden there, a tide of feelings swamped him. His thoughts flew to Kandi and he stiffened.

Oh, man! I'm in trouble...

This girl had haunted him from the first day they'd met, had been his reason for making specific choices in his sad, sorry life. Because of her influence, he'd wanted to be a good man, a useful man. Because of her, he'd attained a certain level of satisfaction in his life choices. And because of her, he'd never married.

Though he lived alone, it was his preference. That he'd become a workaholic... another decision. The only thing he hadn't chosen in the last few years was becoming Blue's master.

He'd never wanted any ties. But his one close friend, the man he'd survived Quantico with, Brian Newton, had decided his area of expertise would be working with the K9 unit. Then Brian found Blue as a pup. He'd trained the German Shepherd everything he'd learned with the FBI program, and though the dog had never been hired by the Feds, he'd been rigorously schooled in every maneuver they used in their manuals.

Two years ago, Brian had been shot on a job and had sent for Dan. While on his deathbed, he'd asked for Dan's promise to keep the dog. Of course, Dan'd given his word and, since then, the two lonely misfits had lived together.

From day one, Dan had treated Blue well, made sure he was walked, fed and that his training never lapsed, but he'd maintained a certain distance and Blue had quickly accepted the difference between master and buddy.

Tonight had been the first time the dog had shown a bit of his old spirit. Though he'd allowed Kandi liberties, he'd refused others, and he hadn't seemed to know how to handle himself. But Dan had understood the animal's quandary completely.

Dan had also been out of his league. Even if he was only acting as the Assistant to the Special Agent in Charge in the Seattle division, he still had to maintain appearances. Getting involved with a junior agent, the only person he'd ever given his heart to, wasn't his style and couldn't be tolerated.

Shit! What next...

Chapter Twenty

"Don't piss me off, Wes. Get your head out of your ass and move it, mister. I want those files on my desk *now*."

Wes and Bobbi clapped. "Whoa! Much better, Kandi. I *almost* believed you." Wes slid his glasses back in place and beamed at her.

Kandi stamped her foot. "Aw, come on. The tone was right. And I made sure my expression couldn't be misconstrued."

"Like I said, you were almost convincing. If only you hadn't handed me donuts while you were chewing my ass. It kinda took the nastiness out of your commands." He laughed, took a bite out of his favorite crueller and winked at Bobbi.

The smell of sweet icing drew Bobbi in and she

reached for her chocolate-covered favorite.

"That's not fair. I always bring you guys donuts on Friday. You should overlook that, not hold it against my academy performance."

Bobbi, chewing happily, now perched on the edge of her desk and wiped the sugar off her face. "Kandicane, you were good. It was believable to anyone who didn't know you."

"Really? I'm getting better, aren't I?"

"You are. That menacing tone worked. You even kept a straight face. Trust me, a perp would take you seriously. Now can I eat my donut?"

No one saw the grinning face of their ASAC until Kandi noticed Dan's reflection in the glass behind Wes. She swivelled, but by then, he'd left, and she felt bereft all over again.

The night before had taken a lot out of her, and this morning she'd made herself promises she intended to keep. *Strictly business!*

Before her coolly professional performance could start, a call came in. They had a jumper. And according to the details that had been passed on, not just any old victim of depression who wanted to end his life; this mixed-up lunatic wanted to take the Mayor with him.

***

Within minutes, the SWAT team had assembled their gear and loaded the SUVs. As usual, Kandi, Bobbi and Wes rode together and arrived at the street where the tall office building had been closed off to the public and the traffic rerouted. Emergency vehicles, including police and an ambulance, had also arrived and the operatives were busy with duties they'd all been trained to handle.

The chaos on the street, hectic in the extreme, had become the norm for Kandi. She thrived on the surge of energy that permeated every authorized person there.

Of course, the media vehicles were crowding in as close as possible. After all, a mayor being taken hostage wasn't a daily occurrence. It was breaking news! Once she appeared, the crowds, forced behind perimeters, became rowdier and the hum of frazzled excitement grew louder.

"Agent Warner, over here."

"What's happening, ma'am?"

"Is it true some sicko is holding the Mayor at gunpoint?"

Voices screamed at her as she passed. With no slowing down in her forward momentum, just a quick smile, she replied, "We've just now arrived and will be assessing the situation, so no further comments at this time. We'll update you as soon as we can, okay?"

Heading to the Sheriff's vehicle, Kandi surveyed the scene. If human beings reacted to danger in such a way out of concern for a fellow citizen, then she'd accept their conduct and understand.

But, sadly, after years of working through these

unhappy events, she'd finally come to realize that most of the folks were mainly driven by a bizarre kind of curiosity. One of her instructors had called their behavior human nature. She didn't get it...

"Hey, Kandi. Glad you were free to handle this crazy. He's threatened to jump and take the Mayor with him. Mayor Wells asked for you personally to settle their dispute, so if you come with me, I'll pass you through."

"Is the Mayor okay?"

"Far as we know. His secretary informed us that the nut-job forced his way into the Mayor's office and she heard a lot of yelling. When the guy and the Mayor left together, all that Mr. Wells asked was for her to call you. By the time the building's security had arrived, the two of them had disappeared. Next thing she knew, they were on the roof."

"Was the man carrying a firearm?"

"She says she didn't see a gun, but he did have something in his pocket that was pointing at the Mayor and it looked like one. Since the Mayor went with him, we have to assume it was a weapon."

Bobbi interrupted, "Did anyone recognize the perp?"

"No. You can question Mayor Well's secretary yourself; we're holding her in the office on the ground floor."

Wes approached and spoke. "I'll get the video

feed from the cameras by the entrance and from this floor too, Kandi. We'll run his face through the face recognition files and see if anything pops. In the meantime, I know there's no talking you out of joining the two on the roof, but at least you'll be wired."

Suddenly, she heard the crowd roar and, rushing to the windows overlooking the plaza, she could see everyone pointing up. Many were covering their mouths as if to hold in gasps of horror.

"Hurry, Wes. I need to get up there now."

"Okay, take off your vest. Here, stick that in your ear so you can hear us too." A few minutes of fumbling made Kandi's anticipation levels hit the roof.

"Come on, Wes."

"Okay, okay. You're ready. Go get 'em, kid." He squeezed her shoulders and turned her in the direction where two SWAT members in full gear were waiting to guide her into the elevator.

***

Just as the elevator door's closed, Dan rushed into the office, his stern expression surprising the others until he toned it down. Anxiety cut into him like sharp glass digging into his entrails and then twisting with enough force to make him sick to his stomach.

With his voice a few notches harsher than he'd meant it to sound, he barked his question. "Where's Agent Warner?"

"Sir, she's just left to go to the Mayor. Not to worry, boss. She knows what she's doin'."

"Maybe with an ordinary lowlife asshole, Agent Snow, but this guy is a sick puppy and she has no idea what she's getting into. I want you to call her off."

Wes grabbed at the speaker in his ear and let out a moan before almost crumbling. He had to lean against the desk, his face deathly white and horror clear in his eyes. "Sorry, sir. But it's too late. The perp just fired at her and I think she's been hit."

Dan felt an explosion building. "You *think* she's been hit? Chrissakes! Has she, or hasn't she?"

"She has..."

Chapter
Twenty-one

"Kandi, say something!" The harsh male voice in her ear sounded furious and she almost didn't answer.

"I'm okay. It's nothing, just a small flesh wound," she whispered to her crew, and then turned her total attention to the two men.

She spoke calmly, not wanting to distress the traumatized man with the gun any more than necessary. "Hey, chill, guy. What are you doing? I came up here risking my life to help you out of this impossible situation, and you shot me."

Having bolted behind a chimney enclosure, Kandi now hunkered down close enough to the action to give her team eyes on everything in the vicinity. Having the camera attached to her vest showed everyone downstairs the layout.

Now they knew where the perp was holding the victim and they could set up their gear accordingly. Two male team members crouched by the outer edge, taking cover from the wall.

The Mayor, his tie askew, white hair blowing in the wind and not an ounce of color in his usually tanned face, sat with his butt on the dirty cement roof. Leaning against a short outer wall, his arms wrapped around his knees, Kandi read the palpable fear on his face and watched his hands scrape and clutch at his thighs.

The perp faced him, with his knees crossed and a gun clutched in his hands. He wore ordinary sweat pants and a jacket and looked almost normal except for the sheen on his pasty skin, the two-day scruff on his face and the excessive agitation his frenzied attitude revealed.

He looked in her direction and waved his gun threateningly at Mayor Wells. "No one wants you here, miss. Go away. Leave us alone or I'll shoot the prick."

"Go away? How can I? I'm a cop. Besides, you shot me. Now you want me to leave the Mayor alone with you?"

"You don't sound like you're dying to me."

Making her voice light, with no judgement, she chuckled. "Well, it wasn't very deep. More like a graze, but it's bleeding a little."

"I didn't mean to shoot you. It was an accident."

"Sorry, friend, but 'I didn't mean to' has never stood up in court as a legitimate defense plea yet. Know what I'm getting at here?"

"Whatever! Look, if you don't leave us alone, I'm going to throw the Mayor off this roof and then jump myself."

"Now why would you do that? Don't you have any more bullets?"

"You're crazy! You know that? What... you *want* me to shoot him?"

"Of course not! I'm just trying to point out that you're talking nonsense and we need to make some sense out of all this. Look, can I come and join you over there, instead of yelling?"

"Why? Why would you take the chance? I could shoot you again."

"Let her come, Mr. Kravitz. Please. She'll help us sort this out," Mayor Wells pleaded, his voice breaking.

Bobbi's tones sounded in Kandi's ear, a bit fragmented but she heard enough to get the drift. "The perp's name is Bernie Kravitz."

"Please, Mr. Kravitz. I can help you sort this out, I know I can."

The man made a disparaging sound. "It must be nice to feel so sure about something, but you have no idea what you're talking about."

"Sir, it's my job. I do know what I'm doing here. You can trust me."

"Yes, please, Bernie, trust her."

Bernie pistol-whipped the Mayor across the face. "You shut up! You don't get to talk. You just get to listen." Taking an audible breath before speaking, he finally asked, "Hey, lady, are you armed?"

"Just with a wire—no weapons." She withdrew her gun and laid it under one of the ledges. Then she showed her hands in the air and stood up so he could see her. "So you know, sir, the crew waiting downstairs will be able to hear everything that's going on."

As if to prove her right, Kandi heard Dan say "No, don't move," and when he knew she'd ignored the order, he swore an incredible string of cuss words that made her eyes widen and fill her with envy. She had no doubt that Bobbi's subsequent chuckle meant to calm troubled waters. "Bet she's got her lipstick."

Shit! I knew I forgot something this morning...

"Okay, you can come forward on one condition; you have to promise me that everything we say gets fed to a local television news channel. I don't care which one."

"Ah... Bernie, that might not be such a good idea." Mayor Wells held his hand to his cheek, but the blood flowed through his fingers and dripped onto his formerly pristine white shirt.

"Maybe not for you, you schmuck. For me, it's the only way."

Stopping the pending argument, Kandi consented. "I can do that." She spoke quietly toward her mic. "Wes, you got that? Can it be fixed up?"

"Sure, I'm on it."

Stepping forward, her hands held high, she spoke, "I'm unarmed, Bernie. I promise." She knelt down by the Mayor and pressed a tissue into his hand. "Okay, we've been patched through. You're breaking news right now." She leaned closer in order for his voice to be heard more clearly. "So... can you tell me why you're doing this, Mr. Kravitz?"

"I want everyone to know just what a rotten bunch our politicians are. We support them, and they're supposed to care about the public, but they really don't give a shit. Not about you or me, just themselves. My story is a travesty, and today I intend to get the justice that's my right as an American citizen."

"I care, Bernie. That's why I'm risking my life to help you." Kandi smiled gently. "Tell me."

Bernie, calmer now that she'd settled him down, started to talk. "Can they hear me?"

Getting affirmation from Wes, Kandi nodded. "Yep, we're live. Just speak up a bit."

With his free hand, Bernie removed his glasses and wiped the perspiration dripping from his face onto his sleeve. He swallowed before speaking. "My son, Zeke, who was a shy kid, a bookworm, was bullied from his first year in high school, the beginning of grade nine. I didn't know about this, neither did his mother, or we would have stepped in. Only he hid it from us. Too ashamed, I guess." Tears gathered in Bernie's eyes. Still clutching his gun, he let it rest on his leg while he swiped at his cheek.

Kandi felt her sympathetic nature kick in, and she spoke gently. "What happened to Zeke?"

"So, he gets an invitation to this party; all the kids in his grade eleven class were invited. But he tells me and his mother, *I'm not going*. Well, my wife, who knows more about his activities than I do, she nags him to go. *Be with your friends, she says. Have some fun for a change instead of locking yourself away with that lousy computer.* I guess to shut her up, he agreed. She insisted on driving him there to make sure he didn't change his mind. My wife can be a bit strong-minded. She told me afterwards that when they pulled up in front of the expensive-looking party house, there were a bunch of the guys hanging out in front of the place. According to her, when they saw Zeke, they were all over him, friendly-like, and urging him to get out of the car."

"I gather it was all a put on."

"Yes, but she didn't know. Last she saw, they had surrounded him, and she drove away. Later that night, we got a call from the police saying they were holding him at the jail, and that we needed to come and make arrangements. That he was in a lot of trouble."

"In jail? What were the charges?"

"Rape of a thirteen-year-old girl." More tears fell and Bernie had trouble speaking.

Giving him a moment, Kandi asked, "I see. How old is your son?"

"He was sixteen. And a virgin, never been with a girl. It was all lies. But they charged him based on the testimony of three other boys. They say he took one of the girls into a bedroom and had sex with her against her will. And that he bragged about it to the rest of the party."

"And you know this isn't true how?"

"Because... Zeke would never force anyone to do anything against their will. He'd certainly never boast about it, he's way too shy for that kind of behavior." Kravitz hesitated as if not sure he should reveal the rest of his spiel, but suddenly he broke. "Oy, vey! My Zeke admitted to me he was gay, and girls scared the hell out of him."

"O-kay. That could make a difference. What did he say happened?"

"He'd said the guys began teasing him from the moment he arrived. He'd decided to hang around for a little while, and then leave and go to a movie so we'd think he'd stayed at the party. Meanwhile, they caught him trying to sneak out and gave him a hard time. First, they force-fed him vodka from one of the bottles. Then they dragged him into a bedroom, pulled down his pants and coerced one of the drunken freshman girls to give him a blowjob while they held him against his will, laughed and took pictures."

"Go on."

"Zeke says this girl was totally out of it too. But they kept giving her more shooters. After she'd finished with him, she fell back on the bed and let the other boys do whatever they wanted. He tried to get them to stop, but they were having too much fun and, drunk out of her mind, she urged them on. Finally, the assholes had enough and left the room. Before leaving, one of the boys punched him and he blacked out. When he came to, he was beside her on the bed, his clothes were half off, and she was hysterical. She charged him with rape."

"I take it the case went to trial?"

"Right... the trial. That's why the Mayor and me had to have this little talk. It was a joke, nothing but a farce. Since she was thirteen and he was three years older, the prosecutor charged Zeke with rape. Considering the girl's condition, her testimony had all been blatant lies, blaming only Zeke. He tried to tell the jury about her drunken state, that it would have been impossible for her to remember what really happened, but no one seemed to care."

"What about the semen from the others? Wasn't she tested with a rape kit?"

"Yes. But the only semen they found was on her clothes and it was Zeke's. The other boys wore condoms."

"What about the rest of the kids at the party?"

"They all swore Zeke had been the only one in

the room with her. Zeke tried to tell the prosecutor the truth, but he didn't want to hear the truth. When I made Zeke tell him he was gay, the man got a distasteful look on his face and marched out without another word. I even went to the school and tried to talk with some of the other kids, asked them to send me the pictures that had been circled around, but their parents threatened to arrest me for harassment and I had to stop."

"What about your own lawyer? Didn't he bargain for a lesser charge?"

"Zeke wouldn't accept a plea. He was as much a victim as the girl. His lawyer tried to approach the prosecutor with the truth, but he would have none of it. There's been too much of this type of behavior in the high schools, and the Mayor here wanted to make an example of any and all culprits. We had no choice but to battle it out in court."

"I gather it didn't go well."

"Not when the prosecution got the other boys into the witness chair and they lied, coerced the victim to lie also, and if that hadn't been bad enough, they tampered with the jury."

"Excuse me? Jury tampering? And you know this to be absolutely true."

"Yes. One of the women on the jury is my wife's hairdresser. Because my wife is a doctor by profession, she's always used her maiden name, so this person didn't tie her to Zeke. She told my wife that many of the jurors had received the Mayor's propaganda leaflets about stopping the rape of young girls."

"What? When did they get these pamphlets?"

"They'd been left at their front doors during the trial. She told my wife that they showed vicious pictures of adolescent girls being forced and had inflamed the jurors so much that they'd decided these kinds of animals needed to be off the streets. And in the case of Zeke, though he hadn't come across as a brutal maniac, they felt if the system dealt with him while he was still young, he wouldn't worsen when he grew up."

Shocked, Kandi's distaste made her feel sick to her stomach. Bernie was right. This was a travesty of justice. *Poor Zeke!*

During this lull, Mayor Wells spoke. "Mr. Kravitz, I admit to trying to curb wild behavior in the high schools and colleges. Some of the stories I've heard led me to believe this need was paramount to the safety of our young girls." He spoke directly to Kandi now so that his voice would be heard. "I am certain that no one in my office would have anything to do with jury tampering. I'll look into Mr. Kravitz's accusations, and if I find out that he is telling the truth, Zeke will get a new trial."

Bernie broke into the mayor's diatribe. "No! No more trials, you asshole. My boy committed suicide last night. He couldn't live with the shame, watching his mother breaking down day after day, knowing the hypocrisy was tearing me up too." Crying hard now, Bernie shoved the gun into the Mayor's stomach. "How in the hell can this society you proudly represent be so fucking screwed up? Tell me so I can understand."

Cringing, trying to hide behind Kandi, the Mayor held out his hand. "Please Mr. Kravitz. Let me right this wrong. I swear I'll do whatever it takes to get to the bottom of it."

"You're a lying son-of-a-bitch."

Kandi leaned forward to catch Bernie's' eye. "He might be, Bernie, but I'm not. Look at me."

Her tear-drenched cheeks and sincere pain showed him that she told only the truth. "Leave it with me, Bernie. I promise to get to the bottom of this. Chances are, we'll find all kinds of evidence to substantiate Zeke's story. I'll make sure it happens, I promise."

Bernie stared at her and finally he lifted the hand without the gun, groping for a connection to her. "You promise?"

She took his hand and squeezed. When he pulled away, she saw a strange kind of resolve enter his expression. Knowing that the next few seconds could make the difference between life, or him doing something really stupid, she added, "On one condition."

Bernie stiffened. "Too late for conditions. Just get the truth out there."

"Only if you hand me the gun. I don't want

anyone getting hurt, Bernie. None of us."

Bernie stood, and she rose with him. "Fine, here's the gun. Now keep your promise."

As he held the gun out toward her, he shoved her slightly. Then flung himself over the roof wall and would have dropped to his death if she hadn't grabbed for his arm and dug in her heels.

Mayor Wells cringed, no help at all, covered his eyes and wailed, "Oh, my Lord..."

Chapter Twenty-two

Kandi grunted. All her effort went into holding onto Bernie. "Mayor, get over here and help me."

Suddenly Bobbi's disjointed voice sounded in her ear, "Kandi, Bernie's wife had a heart attack this morning. They think it was brought on by the kid's suicide. Everyone figured she was a goner and they warned Bernie she wouldn't last the day. But it turns out she's going to make it. They have her in ICU and she's fighting really hard. They want Bernie to get over there and talk her through this, give her strength."

Kandi felt herself being drawn over the ledge; her body weight not enough to offset the dangling man. Throbbing from the strain, her arm's strength failing with every second she gripped Bernie's arm, she derived strength from sheer stubbornness.

Suddenly, Dan appeared, his body wedging hers. "Grab my hand, Bernie. She can't hold you anymore. Let me help."

Kandi called to the struggling man, "Bernie, listen to me. ICU has been listening to the broadcast and they just passed on a message. Your wife is recovering; she's fighting for consciousness. It's a miracle. But they say she needs you there. Let us help you, please, Bernie. You don't want to die."

Tears dripping, her voice wobbling, with a Herculean effort, she yarded him up enough for Dan to grab his now reaching hand.

"Just a bit more, Bernie, we got you, man." Dan swung his top half further over the ledge and snatched at Bernie's belt, using it to pull him to safety. The three ended up on the hard cement in a group, arms entangled, Bernie's sobs the only sound Kandi heard over the wild beating of her heart.

Others from the SWAT team surged forward. They helped Bernie to his feet. Listening to Kandi's hoarse orders—and the go-ahead nod from Dan—uncuffed, they led Bernie to the elevator to take him straight to the ICU before booking him at the precinct.

A stretcher appeared for the Mayor, who gratefully let the attendants take care of him. As they went to pass Kandi, he made them stop and reached for her hand. "I'll see Mr. Kravitz gets a fair trial, Kandi, and this time, I'll be his witness. We'll be in touch. Thank you, young lady."

Once they were out of sight, Kandi laid her head on Dan's shoulder, more distraught than she'd been in a long time. "How can the world be so messed up?"

"I have no idea." His voice, stiff, gravelly with emotion, was the direct opposite of his arms and hands. Wrapping her as close to his body as humanly possible, he softly stroked her hair and rubbed her back. "Goddammit, Kandice Warner. Don't you ever do this to me again."

Chapter
Twenty-three

Bobbi ended up taking Kandi home, orders from the boss. Kandi, finally relaxed, decided she was glad to have the company. Once Bobbi had seen to her superficial wound, the two were lolling in Kandi's contemporary cream, beige and green living room with glasses of wine and leftover sushi, their stocking feet comfortably perched on the furniture.

The high ceiling and full wall of windows, overlooking Seattle's picturesque Elliott Bay, gave an ultra-modern appearance to the room that shouted money. It was the huge, lit crystal fireplace that signified comfort along with luxury.

Doing a quick sweep of the space, Kandi realized that the colorful lime-green pillows and throws she'd diligently shopped for were what gave the area its appearance of cheeriness. *Guess that was time and money well spent!*

Being pleasantly relaxed, she admitted something she usually kept to herself. "Today almost broke my heart, Bobbi."

"I don't doubt it, Cupcake. You were dealing with a sticky situation."

"Bernie really wanted to die. I saw it in his eyes. Once he'd told his story, and trusted me to see his son's name cleared, he had every intention of jumping."

"Yep. None of us doubted it. The poor guy tried hard to make it happen. If it hadn't been for you, he would have dropped, and the crowd would have been satisfied."

"No!" Shocked, Kandi sat forward, and Blue instantly rose from where he'd been guarding the door and started in her direction. "I'll never believe that." She reached out to pet the dog, but he shied from her reach, watchful but determined.

"Of course, you wouldn't. But it's true. Some of those heartless whackos were actually yelling for him to jump."

Kandi shook her head and leaned it against the back of the sofa. "How sad." Blue whined and slowly advanced, his eyes never leaving Kandi but making sure not to get too close to Bobbi.

"What's with this dog, Kandicane? He's a bit frightening. I thought he was going to chew my leg off when I got out of the car."

"Blue's Dan's dog. He wanted me to be guarded after Sam escaped."

"Doesn't he know about this fortress your dad built for you when he found out you were going into the FBI?"

"I showed Dan the security last night when he brought Blue over, but he thinks I'm scatty; doesn't trust me to turn it on."

"And that's because...?"

Kandi grinned self-consciously. "Probably because I didn't have it on when he arrived."

"Ha! The man's not stupid. He knows you're too trusting. In today's world, bad things really do happen to good people, Pollyanna. It's best to stay safe behind locked doors and take precautions."

"After these last few days, I guess I can't argue. But please don't ride me. I already got my weekly lecture from Dan until I couldn't take it anymore."

"What did you do?" Avidly listening, Bobbi reached for her wine, but her eyes never left Kandi's face.

"I cried like a baby."

Resentment appeared in Bobbi's expression and she slammed the glass down again. "He made you cry. That man is the coldest prick I've ever known. He scares the bejesus outta me. Until he gets near you. Then he's like Mr. Hyde turned into a Care Bear."

A giggle escaped, and Kandi quickly suppressed

it. "You're exaggerating."

"I'm not."

Bobbi's words lingered, and Kandi reacted. Warmth swooped in, settling like a sheltering blanket, making her feel all cozy and warm. Until she remembered she had a bone to pick with him. "I get the feeling he thinks I'm not up to my job. That I'm not capable."

"Lot he knows. Without you, we wouldn't be nearly as successful dealing with the criminal elements in this city. Hell, even the Mayor knew to request you today."

Kandi thought about Bobbi's words. "I bet that shocked Mr. Bossy."

"They say he's a workaholic. Therefore, I bet he read all our files. With yours, he'd have seen how effective you are."

"I hope so, because he doesn't trust me, Bobbi. I can tell—"

Growling, Blue flew to his feet and ran to the door. Seconds later, a man's silhouette could be seen in the window. Because of the motion sensors, lights now flooded the yard and revealed his presence, just not his identity.

Chapter
Twenty-four

Kandi, using voice control, gave the house computer orders to lock the outside doors and windows. While Bobbi raced over to where she'd left her jacket and weapon, Blue had different ideas. As the patio door began to slide shut, he leapt out and they could hear his barking becoming hysterical. Male screams broke the night's silence. Then they heard a gunshot followed by a dog's yelp.

"No!" Bobbi's arms prevented Kandi from doing anything foolish. "Blue! It's Blue." Struggling, Kandi fought to break free.

Bobbi whispered. "Stop it! We have to do this properly. Kandicane… where's your gun?"

Cold water in her face wouldn't have drenched

her hysteria more effectively. "In the gun safe. I locked it in the gun safe."

"Let's go." The two girls continued to the hall off the kitchen where Kandi always locked up her weapon once she came through from the garage. The safe looked like an ordinary hall table, but after a panel was slid back and Kandi entered the code, a secret door opened. She reached in and got her gun and lipstick just in case.

They moved in tandem to the front door where Kandi spoke, requesting the computer to unlock only the front door. Once outside, Bobbi swung to the left and did a sweep while Kandi moved forward to the right. In the distance, they heard Blue's whimpering, but nothing else.

Bobbi motioned that she would head toward the driveway to see if there was a vehicle at the end of the road. Kandi nodded and, keeping her gun aimed in front, held securely in both hands, she slowly moved in the direction from where the noise had first been heard.

As she rounded the corner patio, rough hands grabbed her from behind, one covered her mouth. The arms were like steel grips, but it was the threatening voice that made her hesitate before screaming. "Your dog's not dead yet, sugar. Don't make me kill him."

Kandi stopped struggling and nodded.

"Your friend will be back in a few seconds, so we don't have much time."

The grip on her mouth loosened. Heavy breathing an indication of his ramped-up adrenalin, Sam nuzzled her neck from behind and made her cringe. "You even smell like sugar." He groaned. "God, I can't stop thinking about you."

That's it! No more vanilla scented body lotion for me...

"Look, we need to leave now. If you come quietly, I promise not to hurt anyone."

She nodded again and waited for him to direct her. Once they were well away from Blue and Bobbi, she would teach this lunatic a lesson he wouldn't soon forget. But for now, she had no choice but to follow orders.

Chapter
Twenty-five

Dan swung the wheel of his car to head in another direction and turned off the annoying voice on the radio. He'd tried every way he knew how to relax, but after the day they'd just had, he couldn't let go of the ball of fear stuck in his craw that made breathing difficult.

Throughout his profession, he'd managed to keep to himself, do his job and live peacefully. Three days working with Special Agent Kandi Warner and he'd become so tied up in knots, he couldn't function.

The cold prick everyone recognized as Dan Black had been buried under the tenderness that drenched him every time the dizzy broad entered his orbit. This crazy attraction confused the shit outta him and had made concentration impossible. Made sleep a thing of the past and food a fond memory.

Judas Priest! I need to get my head on straight if I'm to do what I'm here for.

Unable to relax, driving through the streets, supposedly heading back to his condo, Dan found himself in Kandi's neighborhood instead.

What the fuck! Man, you got it bad.

He pulled up on her street before the turnoff to her driveway determined to have a straightforward discussion with himself, which, in all probability, would involve misery and name-calling.

Suddenly, the lights around the house's perimeter flashed on. Acting instinctively, he punched on the brakes, pulled over and opened the door. Then he hesitated, fighting off the stupid voices again.

She and Bobbi are probably wandering around the grounds taking Blue for a walk. Give it up, man. Go home, for Chrissakes.

He got back into the car. Sitting, his hands clenching the steering wheel, he braced his head against the backrest and tried to calm the spike in his pulse.

Acting like the cop he was, he scanned the neighborhood. Other than a vehicle parked about a quarter mile up the road, nothing looked out of place. Thinking fresh air would clear his head; he lowered the window... and heard Blue barking ferociously.

Something's wrong! Exiting the car, he removed his gun from its side holster. Then he palmed it between both hands. Keeping it aimed toward the ground, he swiftly moved forward.

A shadow could be seen a few feet ahead of him. He crouched down behind a bush to wait and see who it was. He was glad he'd waited. Bobbi appeared walking slowly, her own gun at the ready.

Something's wrong...

Speaking so as not to frighten her, he whispered. "Detective Carter. What's happening?"

Bobbi stopped and zeroed in on him. She held the gun at the ready, not aimed to shoot, and spoke very softly. "Boss? Is that you?"

"Yeah! I... ah, had to speak to Kandi about something so I decided to stop by. What's going on?" He stood and came over to her so they couldn't be heard.

"We had a prowler. Blue got out and attacked, but we heard shots and we think he took a bullet. Kandi's checking the front, and I wanted to be sure there aren't any others waiting out here."

"Did you call anyone?"

"Didn't have to. The alarm will have kicked in. The police should be here any minute."

"You wait for them. I'm going after Kandi. I didn't see anyone else but there is a vehicle about a quarter mile up the road. Could be the culprit's."

"I'll let the officers know. You okay alone? We

only saw one male."

"Sure." Dan slunk down and made his way to the end of the drive. Following his memory of the night before, he crouched and ran from bush to bush to get to the front of the house where Bobbi said Kandi had gone after Blue.

Rounding the corner, he watched as a black shadow, gun held out in front of it, marched its victim toward the edge of the property. He couldn't identify the male, but he'd know Kandi's figure anywhere. If he recalled rightly, the path they headed for would take them to a fence and then to the road.

He could barely make out Blue's shape on the ground, but a feeble whimper gave him a clue. As the two passed the animal, Blue seemed to gather strength. With a growl that made Dan proud, the dog surged to his feet and went for the man.

Kandi, taking her opportunity, moved faster than he'd ever seen it happen. She whirled around, breaking her captor's hold and set up to kick him in the knees. Before she could make contact, the asshole levelled his gun and aimed it at the dog. "I'll kill him. I don't want to, baby, but I will."

Blue, his strength used up, stumbled to her, thinking to still protect.

"Stay, Blue." Kandi ordered him with a firmness he'd been trained to listen to.

"Good girl. Come with me now."

Dan stepped out of the shadows. "She's not

going anywhere with you, asshole. Drop your gun."

Sam fired in Dan's direction, while Kandi broke from his hold and headed for the trees. Dan fired back but Sam took off, his figure disappearing into the night. Just as Dan decided he'd get Sam at the next bend, Kandi appeared from behind a bush and with a flying tackle, she pushed Sam over.

No! With his heart in his mouth, Dan rushed to where the two bodies, rolling ass-over-tea-kettle, headed straight down a steep incline. By the time he'd gotten to Kandi, she lay unmoving and Sam had disappeared.

When he ran to her side, he saw the large jagged rock under the side of her head. Blood soaked the ground nearby and everything inside him froze. Everything except for the heartbroken sob he couldn't hold back.

Chapter
Twenty-six

Upon waking, Kandi sensed the soreness in her head before she moved. *Yep! Pain. Not good.*

She opened one eye carefully and then the other. It was morning and she was in a smallish room in the hospital. Her father sat in a chair pulled close, and he held her hand while sleeping with his head on her bed cradled by his arms.

Feeling her other hand imprisoned, she carefully looked to the right and there was Dan Black. Only he wasn't asleep. His watchful glare narrowed in on her, and being a coward to the tips of her bare toes, she lowered her eyelids and pretended to still be unconscious.

"Don't even think about it. You opened your eyes. I know you're awake." He squeezed her fingers gently, and his whisper was low enough that it didn't wake her father but harsh enough that she knew he wouldn't back off.

She shuffled across the bed and closer to his side. "I'm still pretty dazed. What happened?"

"I'll tell you what happened. You acted like some heroine in a made-for TV FBI serial. A flying tackle at Sam to stop him getting away is what happened." Dan's tone rose toward the end of his blast and she shushed him.

"*Shuush.* You don't want to wake my dad. Trust me. How did I hurt my head?"

"The bastard flipped you over onto a rock."

"Oh!" She couldn't remember that part. The vision of a furious animal lunging came to her. "Is Blue okay?"

"Yeah. The vet said he'd lost enough blood to warrant a transfusion, but they sewed him up and he'll be fine in a few days."

Worry turned to joy. "I'm so glad."

"Somehow, he'd crawled to where you lay, and until I stopped him, he tried to attack anyone who came too close. Crazy dog."

"He's wonderful. I'm so glad he's not worse." Squeezing his fingers to share her happiness, it delighted her when he returned the gesture. "Did you get him?"

Dan shook his head as if to clear the cobwebs. "Get who? Your dad? No, the Sheriff must have called him."

"Yeah, he's made that part of their deal. Dad pays into their charity every year, and they babysit me and keep him in the loop. It's ridiculous. But, I meant, did you get Sam?"

"Sam? Hell no. After finding you covered in blood sprawled at the bottom of the ravine, I didn't even bother going after the prick."

"Ravine?" She snorted. "You're exaggerating. It's a small sloping hill."

"Which will be levelled out as soon as you're better, sunshine. Now, who's this fellow and why's he holding your hand?"

Oh, oh! They'd woken her dad. She carefully turned his way. "Hi, Pops. How are you?"

"Me? I'm waiting for you to answer my questions."

Dan had let go of her hand and began acting extremely uncomfortable. Not sure how to respond, she decided the truth didn't sound all that bad until after the words were said. "He's my new boss. And he thinks I'm incapable of looking after myself. Remind you of anyone?" *Uh, oh... not good!*

Dan rose to his feet and loomed over the side of her bed. He reached to shake her father's extended hand, and the scowl he sent in her direction left her uncharacteristically annoyed.

"Your daughter takes too many chances, sir. I was just reading her the riot act."

Amazingly, Ben Warner's smile became real,

rather than one of the fake ones he usually bestowed on any man who showed interest in her. "Finally, a good-looker showing gumption besides intelligence. I've been telling my daughter the same thing for years. Don't know why she has to be in the middle of every crazy-assed situation the people in this city get themselves into. First, an armed bank robbery where a bank manager is killed, and the next day she's hanging halfway over the edge of a skyscraper. Now, tonight, she's tackling a killer in our own back yard." He snorted his disapproval. "And you wonder why I'm old before my time."

Feebly, Kandi added, not that anyone was listening, "The building's not a skyscraper."

Before they could argue, the door opened, and a doctor walked in trailed by Bobbi and Wes.

Thank you, Lord... an end to the scolding.

Dan leaned toward her and added. "This isn't over."

Her father squeezed her hand, got up and stepped back. "Oh, yeah! We need to talk, little girl." His nodding head an indication of his seriousness.

While the doctor checked Kandi's chart, Bobbi waved from the side of the room and added, "You scared the hell outta us tonight, Kandicane. I'm so relieved Sam didn't get you."

Wes added, "You gotta slow down, Cupcake. My heart can't handle all this stress."

With her head pounding, feeling adrift on an ocean of censure, Kandi gave the doctor a pleading look and waited for him to dump on her too.

"I'm happy to say you had a good night. Looks like only a slight concussion, Miss Warner. I'll sign the release slip for you this morning."

"No! Please, Doctor; keep me for as long as you want. Don't rush anything on my account." Her feeble smile faded when no one else shared her little joke. She didn't even try to silence the ensuing groans.

As the doctor left the room, a candy striper entered carrying a huge bouquet of red roses... had to be three dozen of the suckers. Tucked under her arm was a fancy decorated box, through the cellophane window of which, sugar-coated candies were seen clearly. Everyone in the room stiffened, except for her father. He looked amused until he sensed the tension.

With authority, Dan held out his hand and the young girl automatically handed him the gift before placing the flowers in the window. Pulling the small envelope off the parcel, a knife suddenly appeared in his hand that he used to slit the edge. Then he passed it to Kandi.

Bobbi handed Kandi some rubber gloves from the box over the sink and being extra careful not to smudge any fingerprints, she slid out the greeting card.

I'm sorry you fell and hit your head, Kandi. Sending

sweets for my sugar!!

Chapter
Twenty-seven

"Dad, stop! I keep telling you, the house is safe. With Blue home now, it's doubly so. You don't have to hang around any longer, and I need to get back to work." Three days of being trailed by both Blue and her dad had almost driven her to take up serious drinking or... or some other vice to relieve tension.

Ben Warner rose from the kitchen stool and went around the counter to where she was fixing him breakfast. His long Jesus robe trailed slightly behind him; on anyone else, it would have looked ridiculous, but on his tall frame, it seemed somehow right. Or maybe it was that Kandi had seen it so many times that it had become normal for him to appear in such a way.

His never-ending anxiety irritated her, but she listened with respect. She adored the man, had all her life. From as far back as she could remember, it had been just her and him, so while growing up he'd been her whole world.

"I'm supposed to ignore what's right in front of my eyes."

"What do you mean? I'm fine now." She'd tried to downplay the significance of the flowers and candy that had been delivered to her in the hospital, but her dad was a sly old coot and wasn't easily fooled.

"I mean, you have a stalker who's a known killer. And you want me to ignore the danger and go about my life like everything was normal? Are you kidding me?"

Blue rose from where he'd been watching and stood in between them, as if he wasn't sure whether her father's frustration should be allowed. He whined and only her now invited caresses seemed to calm his anxiety.

Ever since Blue had returned from the vet's, he'd been her shadow. Maybe he sensed her inner fear, the worry she couldn't hide, even though she tried so hard. How could she do her job and live her life if she let Sam Dixon get to her?

And having everyone she cared about encircle her so she couldn't breathe didn't cut it either. It was hateful knowing the people who mattered had no faith that she could look after herself. That she was weak.

Hell, she'd wanted to be tougher, hadn't she? So now was the time. She needed to stiffen her backbone and get on with her life. When and if danger confronted her, she'd be ready. Until then, life needed to get back to normal, or as normal as her friends would allow.

"Dad, I love you dearly—"

"I'm not leaving." He crossed his arms, his expression firm.

"But you need to understand—"

"No! You need to understand. Would you leave me alone at a time like this?"

Deciding to pull out the big guns, she let him have it. "You're adding to my problem, Pops. Look, if Sam finds out about you, he wouldn't hesitate to use you to get to me. See? Your being here isn't improving my protection, it's actually the opposite. You're just giving him more ammunition against me. Don't shake your head... I've seen it happen many times."

Ben stopped talking. His face underwent a series of expressions, starting with bullheadedness and ending with sad acceptance. "Blast it, Kandi! You know just how to get your way."

She quickly hugged him and whispered in his ear. "I'm right, Popsicle. Admit it."

He visibly melted when she used his favorite nickname. "Yeah, I know. I'll leave for now. But you have to promise me."

"Anything."

"You'll keep the house's security on constantly, even when you aren't here. And Blue stays with you at all times, even on the job. Dan's given the all-clear."

"Okay... and?"

"You'll let your boss call the shots. No arguing if he wants to put protection on you."

"No doubt you've already insisted." She eyeballed the red flush appearing in his cheeks. "Dad! You can't—"

"You want me to leave? Humor me."

"Fine." Breathing a sigh of relief, Kandi agreed. "Dan can have me wired, tailed, whatever, as long as he doesn't try to stop me from doing my job. I don't want that slime-ball Sam Dixon to change my routine in any way. I'll gladly take precautions but that's it. I need to work, or I'll go seriously over-the-edge whacky."

Chapter
Twenty-eight

Dan strode toward her as she exited the elevator. "Where's Blue?" His eyes didn't look quite so chillingly black today, more like a dark blue with sparks of heat deep within.

She shivered, though it certainly wasn't cold in the office hallway. In fact, her body temperature had risen significantly as soon as he'd appeared. "I dropped him at the vets. It's his last appointment. I can pick him up in an hour."

"Good. From now on, he stays with you. I've cleared it with Fred and he's fine with the arrangement."

"I understand. I'll be glad to have him with me. He's very well trained." She sensed his indecision and waited for him to share.

"If any calls come in, I want to be informed before you leave the building. You're never to be alone. Has the asshole called you yet?"

"No."

"I want to know immediately when he does."

She picked up on his words. No "if" in the equation, but *when he does* came through loud and clear. "Okay." So, Dan figured he'd be calling her too. Dread trickled in and her stomach muscles knotted. "Look, I talked my dad into going back to the commune. Do you think he's safe there? I mean, Sam would have no way of knowing where he lives, right?"

"I doubt it. Your father seems to have always kept a low profile."

"It's because of his inventions. He's been labelled a genius, and there're many industries who'd love to add him to their payrolls. However, they wouldn't stop harassing him and eventually forced him into hiding. After he earned millions for the first company he sold, he's never been interested in their money or their esteem. For him, his tinkering has been more of a challenge of creation, coming up with something completely new he could play with. He's just a kid at heart."

"Yeah – a kid with an IQ way over the norm. I asked him about the security there. Seems he's surrounded by friends. I'm thinking he's safe, but I know the name of a good bodyguard if it would make you feel better until this is over."

She started slowly toward her office and Dan walked alongside. "Pops could afford security, but he'd hate it. Better not push my luck, or he might decide to move back into the house with me." She smiled and playfully shuddered at the same time. "Don't think I could take any more of his protection. You know, he'd begun waiting outside the bathroom door, both him and Blue. It's damned unnerving when a person is used to coming out wrapped only in a towel."

If she expected him to grin and share her joke, he didn't disappoint. But the sparks shooting from his narrowed gaze made her clench her legs in an effort to stop the sudden thrilling sensation, a physical reaction to his heated stare.

Changing her direction, Dan suddenly took her arm and led her to his office instead. "I have some questions for you which the others don't need to hear."

Feeling slightly off-kilter, she nodded and waved to Wes, who'd been expecting her to come up with a new spiel of greeting. This time she had a whopper, but it could wait.

After they entered his office, Dan closed the door and pointed to the chair across from his desk. The vertical blinds were mostly closed, and he pulled the cord all the way, making sure no one could see into the room. Then he perched on the edge of his desk.

"How well do you know Wesley Snow?"

Chapter Twenty-nine

Dan waited for her response and wasn't disappointed. She bristled. Her words were clipped and to the point. "He's one of my team. I'd trust him with my life and have done so many times."

"Doesn't count. It's the job."

"Then, as a friend, I love him dearly. Him, and his wife, Patti. They're good people. Why are you asking me this?" She stood and faced him, moving into his space until his hands itched to touch. The long bouncy curls around her face had been pushed back with some kind of doodads, the blue of the glittery stones in them matching the tones of her searching eyes. They also picked up the color in her pretty shirt with the frills around the collar.

"No reason. Just asking."

"Not good enough. What's going on?"

Damn, this chick had the instincts of a shrewd politician and the guts to tackle him in a way most others—including men—wouldn't dare. "We have proof that vital information is being leaked from our main data base, and we've traced it to this office."

"And because Wes is the most talented on the technical side, you're looking at him."

"Something like that."

"Well, you can move on and check the IT department. There's always people coming and going from there."

"Oh, we're on it. First place we looked. But it isn't being leaked from any of those processors."

"You can tie it to his computer or his laptop? I don't believe it. He wouldn't be that sloppy. He's too smart."

"No. Not the specific devices. You do know, however, that anyone can hack into another's browser if they know the passwords."

"Sure, and we all know how. It was part of our training at Quantico. Which brings me back to, why Wes?"

"Because he has ties to the leader of the gang we're after. First, information has been gathered about these people over the last year which suddenly disappeared. It is, I might add, highly confidential information."

"And second?"

"Two undercover operators have been murdered."

"Again, you haven't answered my question. Why Wes?"

"Lady, you don't give up, do you? What I'm about to tell you is classified. Agreed?"

"Yes."

"Because... we know the leader of the gang has two identities. One is Jorge Lobo, but he's otherwise known as George Lewis. Wes grew up with George in an orphanage and they still keep in touch."

"I've met George a few times. That signifies nothing. Every one of us has a background. Doesn't mean Wes'd breach security and obtain or illegally tamper with FBI files for a childhood friend."

"That's true. But we know the breach came from this office. Besides that, Wes is the only one flagged." He held up his hand to stop her from voicing her next remark. "I know odd flukes happen. But this is too damn coincidental."

"So, you've targeted him. But he couldn't be the culprit. He's one of the best agents in this office."

"Those files were sensitive; they'd been tagged because the data had recently been updated. Look, Kandice, that gang is responsible for smuggling huge shipments of drugs across the border by using drones. These newest drug mules are ideal because they can transport product quickly, drop it down anywhere according to the GPS address, and have less chance of being caught. But we'd been informed by our undercover moles, both now dead, and we had their newest dispatch in our possession telling us where the drugs would be delivered."

"And you intended to move in on the gang?"

"Until those files disappeared. The night after George Lewis was seen drinking in a bar with your friend Wes."

"Shit!"

"Exactly."

"I still don't believe it..."

"Okay, princess, hang on to your fairy-tale illusions, but from now on, I'll need you to keep your eyes open and pass on anything that looks suspicious."

"You mean squeal on my partner."

"Pretty much, yeah!"

Chapter Thirty

Gritting her teeth, Kandi left Dan's office and rather than playing the game with Wes, she waved him off, pretending not to see his disappointment.

In her career, there'd been numerous times when the job had gotten to her. When discovering the fallible tendencies of her fellow humans had had her questioning her line of work. Today could be chalked up as the worst one yet.

Lower than low, she sunk into her chair and dropped her head onto her arms on her desk. A dark fury settled, and it wouldn't be shaken off. She squeezed her eyes shut and tried to swallow the hard ball of anger that had lodged itself in her throat, blocking her airways. Panting short breaths that made her dizzy, she groaned. *Not Wes. No way!*

Bobbi entered, looking uncertain. "I thought I saw you come in here."

Wes ambled in right behind her. "Hey, cookie. Got a greeting for me today?"

When Kandi turned to them, she saw Dan hesitate outside the door, as if unsure whether to join them. Without an ounce of fun in her face, she turned to Wes and said, "Yeah, I got one for you. Someone is fucking with a friend of mine and I'm gonna get to the bottom of it."

"Whoa!" Wes shared a high-five with Bobbi and beamed at her. His proud grin made the twinkle in his eyes appear brighter than normal. "Agent Kandice Warner—now that's what I been talking about. See... what you just said? That was believable."

She stared at Dan who didn't look away, instead waited to hear her next words. "Good, because I meant every son-of-a-bitchin' word."

Suddenly, both Bobbi and Wes's expressions sobered. They looked at each other and then at Kandi. Bobbi moved in closer as if for support and Wes's perplexity became very apparent.

"Kandi?"

Before she could shake off the gloom, the phone rang, and she barked into the receiver, "What?"

"Hey, sugar. Is this a bad time?"

Chapter
Thirty-one

Heart pounding, Kandi gave Dan the nod and he waved everyone into action. Within seconds, Wes had rushed out to his equipment to set up a call intercept so he could track Sam's whereabouts. At the hospital, he'd installed a bugging device app on Kandi's mobile phone and now it was paying off.

Kandi cleared her voice and answered. "Hi. You caught me at a bad time."

"People there with you?"

"Yes."

Sam chuckled. "Don't you ever lie?"

"Not usually. As a kid, I couldn't keep a straight face. Got caught every time, and it always made me feel bad. Finally, I decided I'd remember the truth a lot easier, so I gave it up."

Dan nodded at her while he listened in on another line. His waving meant for her to keep the caller talking, so she added, "And you, Sam. Do you lie?"

"Hell, yeah! A word of advice, baby. Never believe a word I say unless I tell you it's the God's honest truth. One thing my mama taught me: never take his name in vain or attach it to bullshit. And as both you and the good Lord know, I loved my mama."

"I'll remember that. Thank you for the flowers and candy you sent me at the hospital."

"I bet your boys were mad when they didn't find any fingerprints on the card." His laugh grated, and she itched to hang up on him. "Honey, I'm glad to know you're well enough to be back at work. You had me worried. Gotta go, sugar, but you'll be seeing me soon."

The silence at the other end of the line meant he'd ended the connection, but Kandi didn't hang up until Wes came to the door, his downcast expression alerting everyone to bad news. "He bounced the signal too many times for us to pick up his location. Whatever he's using is slick and untraceable."

Bobbi added. "He knew we'd try and pick up his prints off the card. He probably also knew we'd pay the flower shop a visit and get told that he hadn't been there, that the order had been made over the phone and a stolen credit card used. The man's no idiot."

"No." Dan interrupted. "But he is a killer, and you all need to remember that." His concern resonated, and Kandi recognized the inflexibility within the words. "He might be attracted to Kandi, but when she lay there with blood pouring out of her head, he left her and saved his own ass." Dan's cold tone made Kandi shiver. His eyes held a warning that no one in the room could repudiate or ignore. Knowing his message had been received, with a satisfied nod and a telling look at Kandi, he left the room.

Silence lasted for a few seconds while Kandi saw Wes and Bobbi share a what-the-hell-is-going-on look. She'd shared that same message with them many times and felt a bit left out until Bobbi approached and took her hand. "What the hell *is* going on, Kandi?"

As soon as Bobbi questioned her, Kandi became a partner again. First, she eyeballed Bobbi to see her friend's openness and caring. No underhandedness there at all. Leaving Wes till last, apprehension building, she caught his eye and stared.

His dark curls, overly long, covered some of the pudginess of his round face. They gave him an angelic appearance that was totally in opposition to his clever brain and unflappable personality. She'd seen him in all kinds of situations, but not once had he been anything but professional and in control.

"What do you mean? Having a killer stalking me isn't enough for you guys?"

Kandi sighed and rubbed the spot on her head where the tenderness had blossomed into a headache. "I've got to go and pick up Blue. Bobbi, will you come with me? Dan-the-man will be furious if I go off on my own."

"Sure. I'll shut down my computer and get my gear." Bobbi headed out of the room leaving Kandi alone with Wes.

She smiled at Wes and saw the rigidity in his expression diminish. "Hey, partner. Thanks for trying to catch the creep today. It's the first time he's called, but I doubt it'll be the last."

"Not to worry, Kandi. The app can record and send off live phone calls to my website, so I'll be a snooper on all your conversations. So, no kinky stuff." He winked at her. "I also used the bugging device to turn on the microphone. I wanted to pick up any significant noises from the guy's surroundings, but he must have been indoors and in a totally silent room. Maybe we'll get luckier next time."

She moved closer and watched his reaction. Totally open to her, he waited and smiled trustingly. "You're one of the good guys, Wes. I'm so glad we work together."

Not an ounce of regret or shame appeared to mar his openness. He winked and smiled, patted her arm and turned to leave. At the door, he stopped and added, "I bought a box of meaty snacks for Blue. Think it'll stop him from viewing my leg like a giant doggie-treat?"

Chapter
Thirty-two

Bobbi waited until they were in the car to attack. "Okay, pal. What's up with you and the Iceman? He's been working on those old files, pouring over the paperwork since he got here. Gotta say, I thought I was glad when that old fart, Neil, retired, but maybe I'll rethink that."

"Bobbi! Neil Ware was a nice man. Don't look at me like that. He might have been a bit slow about some of the modern technology—"

"Hell, chickie, if that old goat had been any more closed-minded they'd have had to use a crow-bar to open his eyes enough for him to acknowledge that the world had moved on. That technology has changed. We now live in a computer age. I'm just sayin'..."

Laughing felt so good that Kandi couldn't stop, though the guilt made her straighten quickly. "Stop kidding around, Bobbi. At one time, Neil was a sharp agent, good at his job. The man couldn't help being old-fashioned."

"Stuck in the last century, you mean. Obstinate old shit."

"I liked him."

"Yeah, well, you like everybody. My friend, I keep trying to tell you, some folks are just no damn good. You gotta accept that after what's happened over the last few days. Even our new boss is worried about your safety; I could see it a mile away."

Wanting to change the subject, Kandi reverted back to the beginning of the conversation. "So, by calling Dan the Iceman, you're saying you're not a fan?"

"Didn't say that. He demands respect. But for now, I'm withholding judgement on whether he's likable or not. But to get back to the earlier matter, when we left last night, and it was pretty late, he was ensconced in his office, all three monitors lit up and completely surrounded by files. Then when I came in this morning, I'd have sworn he was wearing the same suit and tie but with a different shirt. Makes me wonder if he hung out all night."

Kandi shrugged and could honestly reply, "I have no idea. I haven't been at work for three days."

"I know that. What I want to know is why you went into his office this morning all chipper and normal and came out looking like a vicious beast had taken a big chomp outta your ass."

Kandi laughed at Bobbi's witty way with words. "He read me the riot act about Sam. You know, like I just graduated kindergarten and had no idea how to take care of myself. I swear, the man's blind when it comes to my abilities."

"No. It's not your abilities he's blind to. His fear for you overrides any sensible decisions he'd make for the rest of us. For him, you're different somehow. There's something about you."

Smiling one-sidedly, Kandi added, "I know. He treats me like a rookie, and I hate it."

"Oh, sweetie, don't knock it. If I had a big, strong man hovering over me the way he does with you, I'd drag him in front of a priest so fast, he wouldn't know which bus hit him."

Laughing, Kandi pulled into the veterinarian's parking lot. Instead of replying, she got out and bent down before closing the door. "Don't bother coming in. It shouldn't take more than a few minutes, and I'll have Blue with me. I'll be fine."

Bobbi stopped exiting the car, leaned back and her cell phone instantly appeared. "Okay. I'll be here. Just make sure that dog's in a good mood, 'cause the last time I tried to approach you, he looked at my arm like it was puppy chow. Just sayin'..."

Kandi saw the humor in Bobbi's eyes and didn't respond. Instead, she grinned and hurried into the building.

Four people were in the waiting room, most on their cell phones. According to the name tag on the buxom bosom of the middle-aged receptionist, Lydia seemed happy to see her. "Dr. Vonn has been cooped up with Blue for the last half hour. He won't let me into the room and he has a lot of customers being held up. I'm glad you've finally gotten here, Agent Warner."

"What do you mean he won't let you in?" Alarm buttons were sounding loudly. Kandi pulled the phone from her pocket and texted Bobbi to join her. "Well, I heard a lot of noise and then nothing. When I tried to enter, he yelled for me to stay out and wanted to know what time you'd be in. When I asked him why, he said, never mind, but that I was to send you straight back as soon as you arrived."

As soon as Bobbi appeared, Kandi filled her in on what Lydia had said, and then they quietly asked everyone to leave the premises. Kandi, accepting the vest that Bobbi thrust her way, tiptoed toward the doctor's examining room.

Bobbi grabbed her arm. "Stop, princess. Wait. I called for backup."

"Can't. What if Dr. Vonn's in danger, and they harm him because we decided to delay? I'll be careful, and you're here to cover me. Let's go."

She slunk forward and listened at the door.

Then she pulled her weapon, waiting for Bobbi to do the same. There were no sounds at all which made her even more nervous. Hiding her sweaty hands, she knocked and called out. "Dr. Vonn?"

"Agent Warner? Oh, thank God you're finally here."

Chapter
Thirty-three

"Please. Come in." Dr. Vonn's voice sounded rattled... even desperate.

Kandi shared a look with Bobbi and waved her to the side of the door. "Be careful."

"You too. On three."

"One."

"Two."

"Now." Kandi twisted the handle and let the door fling open from the force of her push. She held her gun out in front and swung it around the space, while Bobbi did the same behind her.

A joyful woof was the response to her entry, and a grateful groan exploded from Dr. Vonn who was skulking on the floor in the corner. A tray of instruments had been knocked down and the vet's white coat looked rumpled, as did his temper.

Head lowered, his bushy eyebrows bunched over eyes full of indignation, he gritted the words to illustrate his unhappiness. "That animal," he spat out, "has kept me in that corner for almost an hour. He wouldn't let me move, nor would he allow anyone else to come into the room. When Lydia tried, his snarling threats convinced me not to push my luck."

Kandi petted her frisky friend. Dr. Vonn's description didn't ring true of the now friendly animal, except that she'd seen Blue in action with her own eyes. "I'm so sorry, Doctor. Blue must have thought you presented a threat to me."

"I have no idea how. I only met you this morning. And he seemed fine with our interactions then."

"True. He did. I can't imagine what spooked him into behaving this way. He's very well trained."

Dan rushed into the office, almost skidding to a stop when he saw no danger. He holstered his weapon, waved off the men behind him and interrupted. "What's going on?" He moved over to give Dr. Vonn a hand up while the other man repeated his explanation.

Taking control, Dan questioned. "Did you have any customers after Agent Warner left today? Probably a man? Someone who might not have had good reason for being here?"

Kandi let Blue go to his master and she moved to

stand near him also. Without understanding why, Dan gave her a feeling of safety, and so she just accepted it as fact.

His commanding presence, which made everyone respect his authority, turned her on and gave her the craziest urge to slip her hand into his and lean her head on his shoulder. Strangely, she knew he'd let her.

The silence in the room reclaimed her attention. His questions had rattled her and she, along with the other two, waited for the doctor's answer.

"Yes, now that you mention it. A man came looking for his lost German Shepherd. He said the dog had been stolen. Told me another customer had seen this dog in my office, and the silly man insisted he had to inspect the animals."

When the annoying doctor seemed to think he'd explained enough, it forced Dan to ask the question everyone wanted to hear the answer to. "Then what happened?"

"Well, now," Dr. Vonn scratched his sideburns. "I told him I didn't have his dog and he should check his sources. Then my next patients arrived and when I looked up from greeting them, he'd disappeared. We were extremely busy earlier, and I had no time for any such nonsense."

Dan stepped forward, his cell phone out in front of him and a photo of Sam showing. "Is this the man who came to see you?"

"No. I don't think so. He looked slightly similar."

Dan flipped through the Dixon boys until the doctor recognized John Dixon, Sam's brother. "Him! He came looking for his dog. Can't say I liked him."

"Neither does Blue. Did you shake hands with him?"

"Well, yes. When he first busted in, he seemed legitimately concerned about his dog and he introduced himself as John Denver. I thought it a bit weird, but these kinds of name-coincidences do happen."

"Names don't matter to Blue, only the smell. He must have gotten Sam's scent off of you after you'd been in close contact with his brother. I'm sorry Blue used his skills this way, but I can assure you, Dr. Vonn, you were never in any danger."

"Easy for you to say! Do you know how hard it is not to move a muscle at my age?"

Chapter
Thirty-four

Dan followed Bobbi and Kandi into the parking lot outside the vet's building, Blue heeling by Kandi without any order from his master. Dan saw her run her fingers over the dog's head and gently caress his ear and felt stupid for the envy that surged.

Kandi smiled at Bobbi. "Did they have video surveillance in the building?"

"Ancient stuff, but yeah, they had four cameras and a DVR. Don't know why they bothered since they had them out of sight of the customers, higher up in the corners. I expect the feed will be grainy."

"Even blurry, we should be able to pick up when Dixon got there. No feed outside though, so no chance of the license number of his vehicle."

Dan cut in, "Damn! I'd hoped we might be able to get a lead from this. Those bastards have disappeared from our radar completely. We've checked all their known associates, last addresses and typical joints where they might hang out, but nothing. It's like the slime slipped through a few of the shadowy cracks and the underworld sealed them up."

Bobbi headed toward the car but when she didn't see Kandi behind her, she turned and waited. "We should head back to the agency and pass this on to the guys in IT. They'll work it over, and if there's anything to see we'll get it from them."

Dan stepped in before Kandi could answer. "I'll bring Agent Warner and Blue with me."

"Okay, see you back at Playland."

Kandi waited until Bobbi drove off and then she asked. "Want me and Bobbi to go in undercover to some of the known joints where they might feel safe?" Kandi waited to hear what her boss would say.

Dan bristled and answered quickly. "Not likely! We've already had officers not involved in the case who've done just that, and it's gotten us nowhere."

"I could try drawing Sam out." Dan sensed she was pricking him on purpose, trying to get a rise. When he saw her eyes light up with determination, he felt his heart drop somewhere in the vicinity of the insoles he wore in his shoes.

"Not a chance in hell, Kandi. We wouldn't purposely put your life at risk, so back down."

Her excitement diminished, and she looked grumpy. "It would work. If he thought he could get to me he'd come out of hiding."

"Sure, and if we didn't stop him in time, you'd disappear along with his brothers, and who the hell knows what he'd do to you? The man's a psycho with egomaniacal tendencies. You wouldn't stand a chance against a cold bastard like him."

"So, what you're saying is, I can't do my job. I'm not good enough. Why don't you just come right out with it?"

Feeling penned in like a cow prodded through a chute to the slaughterhouse, Dan wished himself anywhere but standing in front of the one woman who made him vulnerable. Arguing was the last thing on his mind. All he wanted to do was kiss her, taste her again. Feel that pouty mouth and those soft lips respond to his needs.

The twitching skin under his eye signalled the time for backing off, and he tried to do it graciously. "Agent Warner, you are a good officer, maybe one of the best at what you do, and that is to make people understand that you care so they stop resisting."

"But..."

"There is no but."

"Oh, I beg to differ." Her hands gripped her hips. "But..."

He tried to look away and couldn't. Her blue gems, sparkling with exasperation, kept him enthralled and forced him closer. The hair she sometimes wore up in a barrette thing on the top of her head lay scattered around her shoulders, the waves catching a glint of sunlight from behind the gathering clouds. "But... I couldn't breathe if that son-of-a-bitch got his hands on you. So, don't ask me to go there, Kandi. Just don't." When had he tugged her to his body? He didn't know, but suddenly she was in his arms and he held her tightly.

He heard her sigh and then she snuggled in close, resting her face against his chest, her hands behind his back, patting.

Oh, for Crissakes! She was soothing him like a child. And it felt exactly like what he needed. But only until the exotic scent from her shampoo filled his nostrils. Detonated, his libido took over and control snapped.

Unsatisfied, he pulled away and, taking her arm, he walked her to the car and opened the door. Before she could bend her body into the seat, he put his hands into her curls, lifted her face and raging with hunger, he took her lips.

Starving, he kissed her until she whimpered, and he heard Blue voice his own dislike of the treatment—his growl a warning. Sanity slowly returning, he stopped the harsh treatment and changed the kiss into a soft tenderness that she seemed to need—or was it for his sake?

Eyes glowing, she whispered into his throat, "Why did you stop?"

He couldn't hold back the groaning sigh. "Blue's warning only lasts for a few seconds. Then he follows it with action."

Chapter
Thirty-five

All the way back to the agency, Kandi tried not to stare at the man who'd left her reeling. How could he kiss her in such a way and still look so blasted calm? Where was the fairness? When his generous soft lips had touched hers, an explosion had taken place in her gut, just like when cars blow up in action movies, all fire and heat with a blast that stops the world. How the hell was she supposed to act now?

Thankful for Blue, who sat in the back, regal and watchful, she fussed over him, and in too short a time they had arrived at the office. Thanking him for opening the door, Kandi refused to let Dan see her discomfort. She and the dog headed to her own area, and she slumped into her chair.

Why the hell did life have to get so complicated? That man's power over her had become a game-changer. Never before had someone else's limitations restricted her from following her own path. Even her dad's. He'd begged her not to join the FBI, and though she'd hated to see him fret, becoming an agent had been her goal ever since she'd been a youngster.

An incident that had happened when she'd been around eleven had cemented her choice to never give another person the power to frighten her. Now, looking back, she could see its insignificance, but at the time it had seemed huge.

The day she'd turned eleven, her father had finally given her permission to use public transportation to get to her school. Feeling proud that she had earned the responsibility, she'd revelled in her new freedom. Living alone with only a male for influence, and one who worked eighteen hours a day, by eleven years old, caring for herself and being independent came naturally.

Every person she knew, she liked, and they all seemed to like her. Her world was good, and she'd felt safe. But without any warning, her balloon had burst one morning when a bully had tried giving her a hard time.

She hadn't had the ability to deal with the sneering misguided soul, but an older boy who rode the same bus every day hadn't had that problem. She'd never forgotten the overwhelming, sickening panic or the relief when someone else had dealt with what she couldn't handle.

Though she'd never gotten his name, every morning she'd smiled her hello at her new hero. Withdrawn, he'd ignored her until the incident, and though he hadn't allowed conversation afterward, his presence, shy nods and the occasional smile had lit her heart and made her world safer.

But it'd nagged—this dependence, this need of support. She'd found herself watching for him. Then, the one morning he hadn't shown up, panic had ridden inside her all the way to school. She'd not only worried as to what had become of him, but she'd feared everyone near her. It'd left her disgusted with weak little Kandice Warner. That day, a pivotal moment in her life, she'd made up her mind to become a person who saved others, rather than be a victim herself.

Her father—this being one of the few times he'd picked up on anything—had seen her sadness, her dejected mood, and had decided from then on, he'd be driving her to school every morning. She'd no longer ridden the bus, and she'd often wondered what had happened to her shaggy-haired champion with the sad eyes and bruises.

Deep in her zone, when her phone rang, she almost ignored the irritation, not something she'd ever contemplated before. Finally, she pulled out the cell to see Bobbi's number flashing on the screen.

"Hey, Bobbi, did you stop for lunch?"

"Hi, there, sugar. No, Bobbi got held up by me. And... if you want to see her alive again, you will do exactly as I tell you."

Everything in the room started to spin. Sickness roiled in Kandi's stomach, and her gag reflex kicked in. "Have you hurt her?"

"Of course not. Look, this is between you and me. You involve anyone else and she's dead. You bring that fucking dog and it's dead. I want you. Just you! Then we let your friend go, and you and me, we take a little trip together. I'm thinking Mexico."

"You need to put her on the phone. I want to talk to her."

He chuckled. "Knew you'd insist. Here she is."

Bobbi's voice came through, pain palpable. "Don't listen, Kan—."

"Guess she doesn't want you, but I feel the opposite. I can't wait until we're together."

"Where do you want me to come?" The same dread Kandi had experienced as a child washed over her now. It was as if she'd known all her life that this moment would happen, a kind of premonition.

"Now that's my girl. I knew you couldn't let your friend down. I told Michael and he laughed. Said as how you'd never purposely put yourself in danger. See, I knew different."

"Guess you were right, Sam."

"I never doubted it for a second. I felt the connection, same as you did. We're meant to spend time together, get to know each other. Mama would have wanted me to find a girl like you." His rambling dismayed her, but she listened carefully. There was an indistinct sound in the background, but she had no idea what it signified.

"Where and when?"

"Now. Just come up the sidewalk on the west corner and a car will be there to pick you up."

"Okay."

"No wires, sweetheart. You know I'll have to search you."

"No wires, Sam. Just promise me one thing."

"Anything, baby."

"If I come to you, you'll let Bobbi go."

"Sure, sugar. I promise."

"Say honest to God."

"Don't you trust me?"

"You told me yourself you lie. How can I trust you unless you swear properly?"

The chuckle that came over the phone made the skin on her body pebble like it would if she'd walked naked into a cold storage.

"As God's my witness, I'll let her go."

"Alive."

"Yes."

"Then, I'll see you shortly."

Chapter
Thirty-six

Oh, God! Now what? She bent over, her muscles so tight; she wondered if her backbone would shatter. Blue, sensing her reaction to the phone call, moved as close as possible, his agitated whines tearing at her heart. She lowered her forehead against his and ran her hands over his trembling sides; the shivering throughout his muscles a pure indication that he knew something wasn't right.

Blue! He won't let me leave without him. She rose and made him follow her to the ladies' room and led him inside one of the stalls. His eyes questioned and his whines pleaded, but then he obeyed her orders to lie down and be quiet. When he heard the door close, he whined once more. But after her warning, he stopped and all was quiet.

Returning to her office, she collapsed again, fisted her hands and thumped her knees to stop the deluge of tears. Eyes clenched, she bowed her head, her long curls streaming to the floor. *Are you satisfied now? Here's your chance to prove to everyone how fucking brave you are, and all you want is that teenage boy to appear and take care of everything. Time to grow up, Kandicane...*

Straightening, she forced her mind to think of the details. Suddenly swamped with ideas, she sped up her preparations. First, she retrieved her burner cell phone and tucked it into her pocket, then hid her regular one in the boots she now stepped into, a pair she left in the office to wear for certain assignments.

Next, she tied her hair back and layered her clothing. Fitting into her Kevlar vest, she pulled another jacket over it so none of her colleagues would ask what was up.

She patted her pocket and made sure the lipstick tube there had been refilled, and then she added the eyebrow pencil her father had just presented her with, the one with the bottom compartment where a certain chemical compound was hidden.

When questioned about the substance, Ben had smiled in an evil way and warned her not to touch it or especially drink it. But if it was to be added into a criminal's food or drink, someone she wanted to put out of commission, this would certainly do the trick.

Sauntering out of her office, careful not to bring any unwanted attention to herself, she noticed Wes wasn't at his desk. She glanced toward Dan's windows and saw the two of them deep in conversation. *Good! No questions.*

Finally, she arrived at the spot outside where she was told to be and surveyed the cameras overlooking that specific corner. Wondering why Sam and his brothers would choose such an obviously video-covered area, she soon found out.

A city bus pulled up to its stop and her name was called. Swinging around, she saw John Dixon near the driver, waving her on.

Dammit! Sam's family weren't all as stupid as she'd hoped. Now as long as Wes didn't take too long to go back to his desk and check her incoming calls...

Chapter
Thirty-seven

With reluctance, Kandi stepped on board.

"Hi, honey, I figured you'd be here in time for this bus." John Dixon smiled at the driver, nonchalantly took her arm and paid her fare. Then he led her to a seat right beside the back door.

Squished near the window, she checked out the man who looked as if he were enjoying a day sightseeing. He had his phone out front and was taking pictures. "You're Sam's brother?" Even with the bogus FBI ball-cap pulled low over his eyes, she'd recognized him from his mugshots.

"Should I be honored that you know me?"

"Just doing my job. Where's Bobbi? Sam promised if I co-operated, he'd let her go."

"That's between you and him. My role is to get

you to a place where he'll be meeting us."

"You always take risks and do what he says?"

John glared at her, his phony smile gone and only glittering dislike shining from his steely gray eyes. "I don't take orders from Sam. He's a flake. But Michael wants to keep him happy."

"And you do as Michael says. So, what did he tell you?" *Keep him talking, Kandi... He's a human being, and everyone knows, men like to talk about themselves.*

"To be sure you weren't followed. And to get you there in one piece. And... not to hurt you unless you made me."

Kandi raised her hands and jokingly backed away. "Not me, my friend. I'm a wuss when it comes to pain." She smiled and prayed he'd reciprocate.

He didn't. Instead he ignored her and answered the voice coming from the earpiece fixed over his ear. "Yeah, she's here." Silence lasted for some time as he listened and then he spoke again. "There wasn't anyone following. I'm sure." John made a face but nodded. "Right, see you soon."

"What did he say?"

"Never mind. Just do as I tell you until we get off the bus, and everything will be fine. If you mess with me, I'll make sure you regret it." His cold stare and mean disposition didn't bode well for her nicey-nice attitude being effective. But she had to try. At this point, words were all she had going for her.

"Look, I'm only here because Sam swears he'll hurt someone I care about. I'll do whatever it takes for that not to happen, even follow your orders."

John's eyebrow lifted, and he shook his head as if to clear it. "Why the hell would you put yourself at risk for someone else? I mean, it's not like the old West where the good guys won in the end. You know that, right?"

"Of course."

"Then why are you even here? Is this Bobbi family, or a girlfriend or something?"

"No. She's my partner at work. And she's a good woman. Has a kid she's raising alone, a mortgage she'll never pay off and a heart of gold. She's my best friend and I owe her."

"With your life?"

That stopped Kandi dead. Put so bluntly, it brought home the danger she'd purposely stepped into without any team in the wings to back her up. A question hovered between them and she put it into words. "So, you figure I'm going to die?"

"Look, when Sam wants something, he gets it and he keeps it. Until the newness wears off. Then he throws it away, if you get my meaning."

Shivering from the words as much as his callous tone, she shrugged. "He promised."

"Ha! His promises aren't worth the spit he uses to tell them. Come on. We're here." He wrenched her arm so she would stand, and then he frog-marched her off the bus in front of him.

Just after the bus pulled away from the stop, Sam appeared from the doorway of a store and strolled over. "Hi, sugar! I thought you'd never get here."

Chapter Thirty-eight

Feeling the walls of her fear starting to close in, she pulled a weak smile from her arsenal and answered. "Hey, Sam, long time, no see."

"Ain't that the truth? Come with me and John, and we'll get you home real soon. But first, we need to make sure you aren't carrying."

He pulled her close in an embrace, running his hands over her body like he owned it. His cold fingers searched crevices he had no right to, and he even forced his hand up and under her loosened vest so he could make sure she wasn't wearing a wire either front or back.

When he reached the mounds of her breasts, he lingered and squeezed. She came close to kneeing him in the nuts but refrained. Bobbi meant too much. Her safety overcame a few seconds of revulsion.

Once he found the phone in her pocket, he passed it to John who stomped on it before tossing it in the gutter. Next, he pulled out her lipstick and eyeliner, grinned and put both back. Finally, he turned her in the direction he wanted her to go.

Imprisoned by his arm around her back, she walked alongside him for a few winding blocks. It disturbed her that they didn't seem to mind her knowing the direction they were going. If it was to a hide-out, they weren't bothered she'd now have the address. But that small detail didn't bring her comfort; quite the opposite.

Eventually, the scent of the ocean teased her nostrils and she knew they were very close. Sure enough, Sam led her to the dock where a larger fishing boat that had seen better days was moored.

Scanning the area for any signs of life as they approached the vessel, disappointment hit her hard. No one was paying any attention to them. The few people she saw out on their boats were minding their own business. They didn't know her, and they sure as hell didn't care. Hoping to meet up with at least one person wandering around, so she could make eye contact and leave an impression in case they were later questioned, didn't happen.

Then she saw an older man one dock over sitting on his deck and cleaning traps. Purposely, she sent him a loud greeting. "Lovely day, sir. Nice weather to be working outside." The tightening from Sam's arm dissuaded her from taking it any further.

The grandpa-like character acknowledged her greeting with a desultory wave, but never looked up which was disappointing.

Deciding she couldn't rely on anyone else, she played out the scene and hoped it would attract some interest. "Where's Bobbi?"

"She's waiting for you on-board like I promised. Come on, baby. You've been a good girl so far, don't mess up now."

She stood her ground, refusing to step onto the gangplank. "You promised if I came, you'd let her go, swore God's honor."

John looked astonished and broke into their argument. "You stupid asshole, you swore to let the bitch go? Are you crazy? She can ID all of us, you know that."

"Yeah, but a promise is sacred. Come on now. Sugar, get on board and you can see for yourself that Bobbi isn't harmed, well, not too badly anyway. She resisted us, and we were forced to get a little rough, but man, that bitch can kick."

John shoved Kandi from behind, and she had no alternative but to do as she was told. Until she knew that Bobbi was safe, she'd play their game and pray that Wes had gotten back to his desk.

Chapter
Thirty-nine

Dan had called Wes into his office and, without grilling him like a prisoner; he'd been prying information from him for over an hour. His explanation to Wes of, "I'm just trying to get to know my crew a little better, in a more personal way," hadn't set off any alarms. If Wes's comfortable demeanor told the truth, he seemed to be taking it as a good sign, that his new boss was wanting to get chummy, and seemed more than willing to share.

Dan started with obvious career questions and then worked his way onto the more personal. "So, Wes, tell me about where you grew up?"

"I've lived most of my life in Seattle, except during my training and for that short furlough in

Washington when I worked for the bureau there. I didn't like the... shall we say, politics that went on in that city, and couldn't wait to transfer back to the northwest."

"You're married." Dan had picked up and opened a file as if he needed to look up information which he'd actually been studying for days.

"True. I met my wife during those two years in Washington. Her father is with the agency and she'd come to the office to drag the old man out for lunch. We got stuck in the elevator together when the power went out for a short time. One look at her and my heart short-circuited too." Wes laughed at this personal memory.

Dan saw the flare of remembrance lighting up Wes's expression. The man's softened features and eager smile told him clearly that Wes loved his wife.

Not yet willing to share anything about his own past and his reason for being in Seattle, Dan glanced again at the files opened on his desk and continued trying to prize out more facts. "I guess you have a lot of friends here, even people you knew back in school."

"Yep, there're a few." Wes pushed his sliding glasses back into place. "I'm sure it says there that I was raised at St. Joseph's. Some of us who were never adopted got to be pretty tight. I'm not saying it's the perfect environment for a kid to grow up in, but it could have been worse."

Dan thought back to his own early years, and the drinking and abuse from a foster father who hated the sight of him. He shut that door before the memories could bring the usual reaction. *Too late.* His gut tightened and the bile rose, forcing him to grab for the bottle of water on the desk and swig a few mouthfuls. "How about getting fostered?"

"I was shipped out to a few foster families, but they never lasted for long. Most only wanted the extra monthly income and not the responsibility of locking after a needy kid. I was lucky, though; the people who took me in might have been insensitive, but they were never brutal. Some of the other guys had a completely different experience."

"Oh? The system dropped the ball, did it?" Dan snickered in a way to let Wes know he wasn't surprised.

"Yeah, like completely. One of my closest friends, a guy who used to save me from the bullies—and trust me, even though we were all in the same boat, there were still bullies—his treatment from one foster family was inhumane. Thankfully, he was taken away from the creeps but not in time to stop him from being brutalized. He was never the same after that. To this day, he's as hard as they come, except when he's with a few of us from the home. Poor man likes to catch up on old times periodically, but my wife doesn't particularly like him, so we're forced into spending a boy's night out."

Interest peaked, and playing along, bullshitting his way through the fog, Dan smiled. "I know what you mean. I had a girlfriend once who wouldn't come to the beer nights us Fed boys would have periodically. Said we were too wild for her. Guess we were. Some of the guys didn't know when to plug in the stopper, and they'd go too far with their stories."

Wes grinned. "Women sure can be sensitive. Thankfully, I'm working with two of the best. Neither Bobbi nor Kandi give me a hard time when I slip up and forget they're ladies."

"You like working with them." Dan didn't pose it as a question. He knew by the way Wes lit up. His pride in his team shone through.

"Those gals are the two smartest agents in this whole division. They work hard and will go all the way for each other and for me. Can't ask for more—not in a job like ours. Speaking of the ladies, I haven't seen either of them since they left to pick up Blue."

As if Blue had heard his name being spoken, a howl sounded in the distance and both men lurched to attention. Dan swooped to the door with Wes right behind him. Chasing down the sound, Dan headed along the hallway and spied one of the other female agents coming from the bathroom and being chased by a distressed animal who then raced into Kandi's office.

"What happened?" Dan stopped the woman, demanding an explanation.

"Hell, I don't know, sir. I just went to use the bathroom, and as soon as I opened the door, the dog started going berserk. Someone had shut him into one of the stalls. Talk about crazy! He scared me so much; I hesitated to let him out."

"No. It's good that you did. Thanks." Dan nodded at her and followed Wes to his empty desk. The drumming inside his chest made breathing difficult and worry began nibbling at his calm. "Where the hell has that woman gone now?"

Chapter Forty

Sweat gathered on Dan's body and his tie had to be loosened before he choked. *Shit! Shit! SHIT!* He wanted to hit something or someone... preferably that son-of-a-bitch, Sam Dixon. He went to the main office where a frantic Wes was all action and intense resolve.

"I've picked up the GPS signal from her cell." Wes slid his phone into his pocket, grabbed his weapon, his vest and the FBI garment he usually wore. He pushed the alarm for the SWAT team and gave them the coordinates he'd noted and her newest number so they could track her as well.

Dan high-tailed it to his desk to retrieve his weapon and skidded back to join Wes.

"Boss, SWAT's on their way. From what I can

make out, she's at the Bell Harbor Marina."

"You listened to her messages?"

"Of course. I should have been monitoring them all along, dammit! But I left my phone at my desk when I went into your office." Wes looked fed up with himself, and it came through clearly when he added, "I fucking do that all the time, forget my phone. Shit! When will I ever learn?" Wes held out the offending article, clicked open a call and handed it to Dan. "She's gone to Sam like a sacrificial lamb, an offering to save Bobbi's life."

Wes's desk phone lit up. Wes answered and then pushed the speaker so Dan could hear the report himself. Officer Harvey's angry voice came through with more bad news.

"Looks to me like Agent Carter has run into a problem. Got a call about a woman being abducted. When we arrived, we found her vehicle abandoned outside a convenience store. From the look of things, she gave them a hard time. There's blood and signs that a struggle took place. Our men are all over it right now and we'll keep you updated."

Wes responded, his voice unnaturally low. "Thanks, Harv. Get back to me with anything you can find out."

"Checking the vids right now. I'll send them on to your e-mail. And Wes, any help we can be in this situation, every man with me is willing to do what it takes to get Bobbi back."

"Okay, good. Just so you know, Kandi went after Bobbi. Looks like they have her too."

"Oh, shit! Well that goes double then. Anything! You call, we'll come."

"Thanks, man. I'll keep you updated." Wes hung up and turned to Dan. "What can I say? They love her."

"Christ Almighty!" Almost spitting the words, he answered, "Your *Cookie-cake* will be the death of me yet."

"It's Cupcake."

"I don't care what the fuck it is! The woman's a menace." Releasing tension with yelling wasn't Dan's way, and he cut off the rant.

His twitching eyelid had begun its stupid aggravation again and he rubbed away at it. "Why in the hell didn't she come to me? Giving herself up for Bobbi just puts them both in danger."

"Yeah, well... why in the hell didn't I think of them nabbing Bobbi? Shit, the wife tells me we're going to have a baby and all reason fucks off. Man, I'm so stupid."

Dan stiffened. "A baby?"

Wes's grin only lasted for a few seconds. "Uh, huh! Go figure, me, Wesley Snow, is going to be a daddy." He shook off the sappiness and got serious again. "I guess they nabbed Bobbi after she left the vet's and headed back to the bureau. I'm so pissed at myself for not seeing this possibility."

"I never thought of that either. One good thing

though; it sounds like Bobbi's still alive. And maybe they haven't found Kandi's phone yet and she's still wearing it."

Wes's face lit up and he pushed past Dan, rushed into her office and ripped open the desk drawer. "That's my girl!"

Dan and Blue followed. "What?"

"I gave her a burner phone some time ago and told her to use it if she ever needed to have a phone that could be tossed. I think she has that one, and just maybe, they'll take it away and she'll have hidden her own. It's a specialty her dad made for her, tiny and slim." Next, Wes checked her cabinet and crowed. "Oh, yeah! She's wearing her boots and I have no doubt it's safely tucked away."

Pride swamped Dan before he asked, "She'd also take her lipstick, wouldn't she?"

"Of course. That chick never goes anywhere without it." Wes's face brightened, and his posture changed. "Let's go. We'll bring Blue. He'll be able to find her even if we can't."

"Hell, I don't think he'd let us leave him behind." Dan pointed to the dog waiting at the elevator. Blue's whole body quivered with the need to be moving, in service, finding his new best friend, his beloved mistress.

Chapter
Forty-one

As soon as she stepped on board, Kandi pushed away from Sam and gave him a questioning glare. "No more fooling around, Sam. I want to see my partner."

"Okay! Okay, calm down. A promise is a promise."

"You said you'd let her go."

"Hey, don't piss me off, baby. I remember what I said. She's in here." Opening the door, he led the way into a main room walled with golden wood panels and windows covered by heavy black drapes—now closed. Continuing further, he unlocked another small room where she found Bobbi curled up on the floor in the corner. Her beautiful black face, swollen from multiple bruises, looked painful, plus a cut on her mouth still seeped blood.

"Bobbi!" Kandi rushed to her side and dropped on her knees. The door being slammed behind caught her attention, and she heard the lock being turned. An unfamiliar male voice full of contempt spoke loudly. "Now can we go, Sam?"

"Yeah. We're good. Let's fuck off."

She jumped to her feet and pounded hard. "Sam, you have to leave Bobbi here."

His voice came through loud and clear. "No, sugar, I don't. I said I'd let her go, and I will. But I didn't specify where. Now just be a good little girl and behave."

Bobbi spoke, calling her back. "He has no intention of letting me go. You should know that. He's been playing with you."

"Oh, he'll let you go alright. Please don't worry, Bobbi. He promised. I believed him. He swore 'honest to God,' and said when he did that, he'd never lie."

Bobbi shook her head, her expression playfully sad. "What are we gonna do about you, Cupcake? You just won't believe that some people are purely rotten through and through."

From the sound of the motor, they were pulling out of the marina and their chances of rescue were looking less likely by the moment. Thankful that Sam hadn't searched her thoroughly; Kandi slipped the phone from her boot and texted their location.

The message she got back brightened her spirits and she shared it with Bobbi. "They're closing in on the area now and have Search and Rescue on standby. They'll be after us as soon as they can. How are you feeling?"

"I think they busted one of my ribs. Them boys sure do like to kick... assholes."

"I'm so sorry they used you as bait. Once Dad left, I should have known Sam would still go after someone I care about."

Bobbi grimaced and tried to straighten. A groan escaped, and she grunted a cuss word and then another. "Bastards didn't like Sam demanding they bring you along. I overheard them. Michael had fought to leave right after the heist failed, and Sam wouldn't budge. Said they could use you as a hostage if they needed to, but he wasn't leaving Seattle without you."

"Guess I made quite an impression." Playfully, to lighten the tension, Kandi made a goofy face and then pulled the cushion from a chair and stuffed it behind Bobbi's back. "What can I do to make it less painful?" Hearing the roar of the boat's motor being shoved into a high gear, they were warned they'd exited the harbor and were most likely in open water. "Who all is on board?"

"John and Michael were the two that grabbed me. Of course, Sam is here and us two. I think that's it."

Kandi texted the information to Wes and quickly hid her phone again in case someone came in. Searching the small space for a weapon proved futile, so she settled near Bobbi.

"Don't waste your energy. I combed the room myself. There's only the bunk and chair, not even a mirror to break. This boat is a working craft, not a luxury liner."

Kandi smiled, checked the incoming text that said: *Got it. Hold on. We're coming.* And then watched horrified as the message froze and the bars disappeared. "Dammit! I've lost mobile data. No signal so far out to sea. Can they still track the phone?"

"I don't know." Bobbi's voice seemed weaker, and panic ate away at Kandi's normal calm. She checked the window again and could see a small island off to the left. The boat slowed down and suddenly the door opened and John and Sam filled the room, their size shrinking the space.

John pushed Kandi at Sam and then he aimed his gun at Bobbi. "Get up."

Bobbi struggled to her feet and tried to pull away, but her strength wasn't up to stopping him from dragging her from the room.

Kandi locked in Sam's bruising arms, distress weakening her voice, struggled too. "Sam, what are you doing? Where is he taking Agent Carter?"

"I'm just keeping my promises, sugar. I said I'd let her go, and I'm gonna do exactly that."

"What, here? In the middle of the ocean?"

"Hell, there's an island not half a mile from here. She can swim, can't she?"

"No!" Horror made Kandi scream the negative. "No, she can't swim. Your brutal brother broke her ribs. How the hell can you expect her to swim? You swore, honest to God, you'd let her go."

"Hell, bitch, I'm keeping my promise, ain't I?" Anger rose in Sam's voice, and he tried to push her away.

Clinging, begging, tears streaming, she tried to follow Bobbi. "But, you swore you'd let her go *alive*."

"Fuck, lady, she's alive. And I never swore to God she'd stay that way. I never did that. Think back and you'll know I didn't." Before Kandi could reach in her pocket for a weapon she could use, Sam wrapped his arms around her again and tried to push her down on the bottom bunk. She wriggled until she broke free and ran to the corner by the window. In the distance, she heard a scream and a splash and then the motor revved up and the boat swung away.

Oh, God, no!

Before Bobbi's fate registered fully, he came at her, his intentions lighting up the lascivious gleam in his smoky eyes. His voice lowered to a sexy tone, and he spread his hands. "Look, sugar. I've treated you good, better than anyone else I've ever known. But... it's time to pay the piper, doll. Come 'ere and be nice to old Sam. If you behave, you'll be my princess. But listen carefully; I'm a mean son-of-a-bitch if you piss me off."

Hate blossomed and filled her completely. She'd never wanted to kill another human being before, but this man, this evil scumbag, deserved to eat a bullet.

Filled with revenge, her brain scurried over all her options like a mouse in a maze. Thinking quickly and ignoring the yearning to use her lipstick now and get in as many licks as she could before he killed her, she stood with her head down, appearing broken, tears streaming and refused to look his way.

"*Fuck!*" He started to reach for her and instead, he picked up the chair and slammed it into the wall, breaking it apart. Fury drove him to hit the bedpost, but for some strange reason—not her.

Instead, he pinched her arm between his callous fingers and dragged her to the galley. "If you don't want to be dumped out like your friend, sugar, you'll behave and cook some food for us tonight. The boys are hungry. Only reason they let me bring you along is so you'd take care of the meals. And, baby. I know you can cook. Checked your Facebook page and turns out you're almost a gourmet. So, we'll be expecting a good dinner. Then afterwards, you and me, we'll try this again. And you better be willing, or maybe I'll just let the boys have at you instead."

Chapter
Forty-two

Dan and Wes screamed into the marina, shut down the siren and quickly met with the emergency team who announced that the boat had left. They'd scanned Kandi's two texts, which said she and Bobbi were together, with three Dixon brothers on board. Then they'd lost her signal. Once it'd cut out, they knew the general direction the old fishing boat had headed in and little else.

Search and Rescue were gearing up and would be there to pick up Dan and Wes as per instructions, but they weren't too optimistic that they'd be able to track the boat unless the brothers used their radio. Regrettably, they didn't expect that to happen.

Dan had organized the helicopter to search the

sound hoping they might get a view of the boat, but they had little information to go on. Other than knowing the boat was being registered as Little Mermaid, it would be surrounded by hundreds of very similar craft. Its colors of gray, white and dirty didn't bode well for them being able to spot the vessel amongst all the others as daylight faded.

Spreading out, questioning everyone at the marina was of little help. The boats nearest to the one the Dixon boys had procured were tied up and shut down, with no one on board.

To make matters worse, they'd discovered the boat's license number from the dock manager, and it turned out that a vessel with the same certificate and description had been reported stolen the week before from a totally different marina.

Going from person to person proved to be a big waste of time. A few people remembered seeing a woman walking with her boyfriend and another man, but no one had paid much attention.

Frustration didn't begin to describe Dan's anxiety. Every horrible crime scene he'd ever witnessed flashed through his mind and drove him nuts. He popped a couple of Tylenol and hoped the drumroll in his head would shut down so he could think.

Every time he pictured Kandice, his golden-haired angel, he couldn't believe those animals had her in their clutches. Who knew what they had planned for her. His only comfort was in knowing that the two girls were together. That Bobbi would give her life to protect her partner.

Suddenly, a mind-picture entered that wouldn't be erased. Kandi, in charge, with her ingenuity that saved the victims in the bank robbery slipped to the forefront of his mind.

Her bravery and intelligence throughout the ordeal with Mayor Wells had turned a horribly sad situation around to where the final outcome had been effective. Dammit, he had to stop undermining that chick. She'd proven to him she was no slouch when it came to thinking on her feet, and he'd have to believe she'd be doing the same thing right now.

Blue whimpered by his side and Dan stroked the agitated animal. "We'll get her back, boy. Come on, we've got a boat trip to make. We're going to find her. Just you wait and see."

Wes approached, his curls twisted in knots from the wind, his glasses at half-mast, but the glow in his eyes deadly calm and focused. "They're ready, boss. I'll go with them and keep you informed on whatever we find."

"Fuck that! I'm coming too. So is Blue." Dan pushed in front of a grinning Wes and made his way on board the Search & Rescue craft. In minutes, the men had cast off and were in open water. Blue ran to the prow, gusts of wind ruffling his fur, his nose twitching, searching.

Chapter
Forty-three

Filled with rage, Kandi worked in the galley, chopping vegetables for a salad while spaghetti sauce cooked on the stove. She'd boiled the noodles and set the table. No one had come into the room while she'd worked, but she knew Sam was sitting outside the entrance, and when she'd looked through the door's window she'd seen his gun beside the empty beer cans on the table along with his laptop.

Without a care in the world, the asshole was playing video games and letting his brothers work the boat. Tall and lean, his body filled the deck chair with a nonchalance that irritated the hell out of her.

Thinking of Bobbi had put her to the floor a

few times, the pain almost unbearable. *Stop! Oh, God! Don't think about it.* If she had any chance in hell to get outside and stick this knife in her hand between Sam's ribs before the others shot her, she wouldn't hesitate.

As it was, adding her father's elixir from her eyebrow capsule to their sauce gave her a huge amount of satisfaction. She just hoped it made them sicker than the dogs they were. As soon as that thought entered, she stomped on it. Hell, she couldn't clump them together with dogs. It would be insulting to Blue.

Realizing the boat's motor had been shut down, she knew they'd be anchored, and smiled. Better still. They'd all come and eat. She went to the door and knocked on the window.

Sam checked and when he saw her standing well back, he entered. Then he held the gun on her and said, "Put the knife on the table and step back."

She did so, pretending to be frightened. "It's ready. Do you want me to dish it up for you?"

He put the knife on the table outside. "Are you going to behave?"

"Yes."

Sam whistled, and the other two brothers appeared and sat at their places. Four spots were set up and Sam put his beer down in front of one. Then he fetched three new cans and passed them around.

The brothers were dressed similarly, in jeans and

vests, though Sam was all in black. Kandi watched the men take their places. Already familiar with John and Sam, Michael, the oldest, was still an enigma to her. The man didn't resemble his two leaner brothers. Fat to the point of being obese, he had neither the good looks nor the personality of his siblings. Instead, he looked unkempt, his beard scruffy and his hair worse.

When he stared at her, disgust became hard to hide and she turned away. Her instinctive urge to accept the good in everyone seemed to have vanished with this family of dysfunctional misfits. Instead, instant hate consumed her and wouldn't go away.

Filling each plate full of spaghetti, she smothered it with sauce and passed the dishes to the men. Lastly, she served herself a small portion and sat at the table where Sam pointed.

The rest waited and watched her until she began to eat and then they did so too. She pushed daintily at the noodles with her fork but the others, too busy to converse, gorged themselves on the sauce and even complimented her on the tasty meal.

"I'm glad you like it." She tried to act pleased and got up to the pot. "More?"

Passing out all three plates with refills, she wished she'd taken more interest in her father's bragging. Praying the herbal poison was fast-acting, she nibbled at her own.

Chapter
Forty-four

Dan was ready to hurt someone if they didn't give him good news soon. No amount of searching of each of the vessels they'd approached had helped them find the one they wanted. And questioning the folks on board had got them nowhere.

With darkness approaching, dread ate away at his optimism. Until, suddenly, Blue let out a bark and dove over the side. A splash followed and brought Dan to the spot instantly.

"What the hell...?" He looked overboard to see Blue swimming toward a dark blur.

"It's just a log? Isn't it?" Wes approached and checked with his flashlight. Quickly one of the Search and Rescue workers held out his night-vision binoculars and they saw that someone had used a piece of floating wood as a raft to cling to.

Not stopping to think about anything but saving Kandi, Dan stripped off his jacket, then his shoes and hit the water before the others even knew his intentions.

Freezing cold, the shock made him rear up before he began swimming in the direction where he'd seen the body. Within seconds, he'd reached Blue scrambling to climb onto the large log. With a shove to the dog's backside, he managed to get himself up and then he pulled around to where they'd seen a person.

In the darkness, he had to turn her head, but he soon recognized Bobbi as the victim. Ignoring the instant jolt of relief, he inspected the way Bobbi had clung to her perch and saw that the smart broad had threaded one sweater sleeve over a protruding branch. It had kept her from being washed away and had most likely saved her life.

"Bobbi, talk to me. Come on, honey. We're going to get you warm in just a few more minutes. Hang on, okay?"

"Y- you came." Laboring, her voice feeble, Bobbi had difficulty opening her eyes. "Ka-Kandi?"

"Don't worry, Bobbi. Everything's going to be fine." Prying her loose from the mossy branch she'd clung to, he then untangled the seaweed her trailing foot had managed to snag. Soon, he had the help of a couple of the boys who'd rigged a floating stretcher.

Once they were all back onboard, with a certain amount of understandable trepidation, Wes rubbed down Blue while Dan stripped. Swathed in a large warming blanket, his questioning look at the crew on board didn't ease his anxiety in the least. They shrugged, their expressions blank.

Bobbi was in bad shape.

Chapter
Forty-five

Kandi watched for the first reactions to her father's elixir and wasn't disappointed. Being the leanest, yet eating the fastest, Sam's face changed first. He grabbed at his stomach and turned to stare at her with suspicious shock on his face. That was about the time his insides rebelled. Before he could reach for his gun, she'd swiped the frying pan off the nearby counter where she'd purposely left it and slammed him in the back of the head.

Whirling quickly, the gun now in her own hand, she pulled out her lipstick tube and let John have it in the face. The poor man didn't know what had hit him, but Michael did. Imprisoned in the corner, he tried feverishly to get the table and his brothers out of the way so he could grab at her. Saliva foamed and drooled from his mouth but still he reached wildly. "Bitch! What the hell have you done?"

Fury driving her, she wheeled around and aimed the gun in his face. "You'd better stop right there, Michael."

"Yeah, like you're gonna shoot me?"

The first bullet went into his leg. "I wouldn't push your luck, asshole. The next one'll put a hole in your ugly face, right between your mean, little, beady eyes."

Michael, writhing with waves of pain, but still blocked behind the nook table, pushed at John and ordered, "Get her, you stupid prick. She's killing us."

John lifted his face from the plate, spaghetti sauce coloring him orange. Searing red and draining tears, his eyes couldn't focus. Senselessly, he tried to reach for her, but his hand fell short. Upchucking... while his stomach emptied the food from the other end, he was totally incapacitated. "Urgph."

"I think that means he's busy right now, Michael. If you don't move, I might not shoot you again. Mind you, when I think of my friend and what you did to her, my finger's itching so bad, it could mistakenly put pressure on the trigger."

Roaring, his rage halted once his mouth overflowed with the contents of his stomach. By now, the stench was making her eyes water and she spun around and headed to the outside. Taking an oar from the floor by the dingy, she shoved it through the handle, successfully locking the brothers into that part of the ship.

Adrenalin used up, she sank to her knees and howled, the animal-like noises coming from her ripping her earlier composure to shreds. There was nothing ladylike about the release of her accumulated fear and sorrow.

Trying to ignore the disgusting sounds she could still hear from the galley, she fought the weakness she was now beginning to experience herself. Forced to her feet, she flew to the side of the boat and heaved the little bit of food she'd swallowed overboard.

She'd eaten miniscule amounts, mostly the noodles, but even the small amount she'd ingested had started to react. Hanging there, totally spent, she tried to gather enough strength to move.

Listening to Michael's howls, she shook off her lethargy and decided to try the radio. As bad as the Dixon brothers were, she was FBI and her prisoners were in need of medical assistance.

Struggling to get to the wheelhouse, she had trouble erasing the earlier ugly scene from her mind. What a horrible vision to remember. Maybe her father was right. Maybe she wasn't cut out to be an agent. And just maybe, in time, she'd get over the pain of losing her best friend.

Chapter Forty-six

It only took them a little while to reconnoiter once Kandi had transmitted her mayday call over the marine-band VHF-FM radio. But now, passed out on the deck, it seemed like only a few minutes before the Search and Rescue craft pulled up alongside her.

Dan, the first person who came aboard, had her in his arms in seconds, and she melted all over him. "Danny! Oh, my Lord, I'm so happy to see you. I never thought I'd—"

"Shush, sweetheart." He passed his hands over her, looking for wounds. "I'm just thankful that you're alive. Did they hurt you?" He held her away from him, but only until she forced her way back into his arms.

"I'm fine. But Bobbi's gone. They... they killed her, threw her overboard. She couldn't swim—" Tearfully, she had to admit her failure in keeping her partner alive. "I tried to stop them, but they wouldn't listen."

"No, sweetheart, we found her. The helicopter took her to the hospital. They should have her there by now. Smart lady clung to a log and thanks to Blue, who spotted her; I think we might have gotten to her in time."

Blue, hearing his name, nudged Kandi's side and by his whining, he seemed unsure of his welcome. That is, until she noticed him.

Bending toward him, she cradled him in her arms and kissed his furry face. And in his own awkward, canine way, he showered her with slobbery kisses, demonstrating his joy at finding her alive.

Dan, kneeling beside her, kept his arm around her back as if he couldn't bear to be parted for even as long as it took for her to comfort Blue.

Meanwhile, members of Search and Rescue had released the door into the galley and their reactions shocked everyone but Kandi. A couple of them backed away, their faces white and their expressions full of revulsion. Calling for masks and gloves, they waited before re-entering.

Seeing the door open, Blue growled and started toward the opening but stopped after a few steps. He violently shook his head and whined pitifully, the stench that was assaulting him probably worse for him than it would be for humans. He returned to guard Kandi and growled low, voicing his disgust.

Kandi stopped one of the medical rescue workers and shared what her father had told her about the remedy for the herbal poison she'd administered. "These three will need a treatment made from charcoal to offset the effects of the toxins"

"We'll see to it, Agent. Thanks for the tip."

Feeling Dan rise, Kandi grabbed his hand and pulled him back. "You might not want to go inside. Those three haven't been well."

Wes, a mask over the lower half of his face and tear streaks from bloodshot eyes running down under the blue fuzzy material, crouched at her side and ruffled her hair, then gave her a half-hug. "You did it, didn't you?"

"Oh, yeah!"

Dan looked perplexed. "Did what?"

Wes looked at Kandi and then at Dan. When it looked like she wouldn't answer, he did instead. "Last year, her dad came up with a fast-acting herbal toxin he figured could be used in our job to incapacitate dangerous criminals."

Dan waited. "And..."

"Seems criminals have rights too. The FBI bigwigs shot him down. But he'd outfitted Kandi with her own vial hidden in a makeup tube, made her promise to use it if she was ever in danger for her life."

Feeling on top of the world from Dan's good news about Bobbi, Kandi added. "Dad was right, Wes. It worked like a hot-damn." She giggled, and the two men laughed — everyone on a high because Bobbi was alive.

Finally, Wes sobered and added, "Don't think we need to drill you on your backbone anymore, Cupcake. I think you just made it to the big leagues."

"Problem is, Wes, I'm not sure it's a place I want to be."

The Search and Rescue captain interrupted. "Your helicopter will be here shortly, sir; they'll be taking Agent Warner to the hospital."

Kandi let Dan and Wes help her to her feet and turned to follow him. Wes held back to get in a few words with his boss. "Hey, *Danny*, you want I should finish up here so you can go with Kandi?"

Reflexes on high, Dan's fist shot out before he could stop it. Only the fact that it was Wes made him cut the power so the doubled-up man shouldn't be in too much pain. Relaxing his facial expression from its usual cold expression to not-so-icy, he answered, "Yeah, Wessie. You do that."

Chapter
Forty-seven

Dan pulled up in front of her house and dimmed the lights. Kandi looked totally exhausted, and his heart ached for her after the ordeal she'd described when they'd debriefed her back at the office. He'd hated that this beautiful soul could have been privy to such a lurid, horrifying experience.

In his opinion, his blond doll, who smelled wonderful now that the nurses had let her shower and given her hospital clothes, should never have had to see or had anything to do with scum like the Dixon brothers.

On the other hand, her reunion at the hospital with Bobbi had been uplifting, even for the hardened man he'd become. In fact, he'd had to turn away. Friendship, such as the one between these two women, was precious, beautiful to see, and he envied them both.

When they'd first arrived at the hospital, the doctors had had good news, and though hypothermia had set in and poor Bobbi would be kept under observation and in treatment for some days, she would make a full recovery.

Breaking out of his fog, he turned and saw Kandi scrunched onto the edge of her seat and curled up as if holding off the cold. "Kandi, honey, are you okay?'

Blue whined from the back seat, and his nose nudged her shoulder.

When she faced him, he saw the tears streaming down her cheeks, and he recognized his sweetheart was totally spent. "I don't want to be alone."

He went around to her side of the vehicle and opened her door, reached in and lifted her in his arms. As per instructions, he used the remote control to turn on the fireplace which left the room with a sensuous glow, both sexy and relaxing.

Trailed by Blue, who he ordered to guard the outside, Dan got her into the house and settled her on the sofa in the living room, pillows piled behind her and a tissue box nearby.

Dan who was totally inept at dealing with a woman's tears, other than they ripped his insides to shreds, knelt beside her and tried smoothing her hair and patting her knee.

Face hidden in her tissues, she blubbered. "I'm

sorry. I'm not usually such a weepy-Cathy but it's all so sad-d-d..." The sob that followed broke his heart, but because he knew it helped the healing process, he wanted her to release the pent-up grief. Sadly, he couldn't erase her memories or switch off her mind. Or ease the pain she'd suffered at the hands of those bastards.

Shit! Shit! SHIT!

"I'm incensed that you had to go through that torture tonight, baby. No wonder you're so upset. Anyone would be devastated, even the most hardened of us."

She lowered her hands and stared at him through long damp eyelashes. Heightened by pools of tears, the intense cobalt of her eyes glowed incandescently and had him catching his breath.

Her hair, newly washed, was bunched in tendrils of gold around her face, softly curling like invitations drawing his itching fingers. He allowed himself the joy of touching.

As she wiped her cheeks, her sigh sounded weak and a little weepy. "It's not what you think."

Absorbed in the satiny touch of her hair, he'd lost his focus and had to force his eyes back to her face. "What isn't? What do you mean?" Being only an insignificant male with little experience of the female mind, he had no idea what she meant.

"It turns out that I'm not as big a softie as I always thought. When the push came, I stepped up. Something I wasn't sure I could do."

He still didn't know where she was going with her rambling. Rather than put a foot wrong or stop her talking, he nodded and encouraged her to continue.

"Wes and Bobbi used to tease me that I was a softie, and that the criminals sensed it and took advantage."

"I know. They made you practice being tougher."

At her questioning look, he admitted. "I heard you rehearsing a few times."

Her smile was weak but sincere. "It was harmless fun. But secretly, I never had faith that, if necessary, I would have the courage to pull the trigger."

"But you did."

"Yes. And you know what? Since I thought they'd killed Bobbi, it wasn't really all that hard."

"Seriously, I'm sure I've never seen three more miserable prisoners than those Dixon boys when you got finished with them." He winked playfully. "Cupcake, you put them through hell." His teasing surprised him. Normally, he didn't relax enough with people to let his wit escape.

"I'm glad," she all but crowed.

"So why the tears?"

"Because of humanity."

"Humanity?" *What?* He hoped his expression hadn't changed, but she totally had him stumped.

"You know—that people could be so sick and

cruel to their fellow man. The fact that they threw a woman into the cold ocean, leaving her to die, and it didn't register on their consciences whatsoever. Not one of them gave a flying fu... ah, damn. How can people be so merciless? Can you tell me that?"

"Oh, baby. I've been asking myself that question since I was a young, helpless boy." He stopped there because he had no answers.

"Helpless? Is that why you decided to be an agent?"

"It's part of the reason. I have a golden-haired angel to thank for my biggest motivation. I'll tell you about her sometime."

She put her soft hand on the side of his face and stroked him gently until he felt whimpers building in his chest like those of his bewitched dog.

"I'd like that." Her soft voice mesmerized him, and it was an invitation he yearned to accept.

Chapter
Forty-eight

Kandi had never felt so cherished. Having this influential giant—one she held in high esteem—kneeling at her side and trying to cheer her up had surely contributed to her loss of dignity.

Enough already — stop with the tears! It was the same lecture she'd applied to everything that happened since, as a scared little girl, she'd ridden the bus to school many years ago. *No more crying. People are different. Everyone has a story. Don't condemn and never judge. Be brave.*

Her usual restraint disappeared. Or maybe she sensed Dan's craving. She didn't know and didn't care. Reaching out, she stroked his cheek, and loved that his face followed her hand as he nudged her to continue.

Swelling with affection, the need to touch and be touched, she slid from the couch into his arms and ignored his shocked exclamation. Cuddling close on his knee, she tucked her face into his neck, inhaled the smell of his hair and skin that still had a faint salty flavor and let herself enjoy the embrace.

Intentions to seek warmth and maybe a bit of gentle affection fled the minute his control broke. Once his lips searched hers, his tongue reaching, claiming, wanting, her mind cleared of everything except to be with this man—be everything he needed and desired.

By his moaning loss of restraint, his stroking hands that trembled as he hugged her to him, she knew she'd somehow become much more important to Dan than a casual fling.

Be honest. You've always known that. This was no casual hook-up. He wanted her. She'd sensed that from the beginning. Once they passed this line, they could never go back. She sensed that too.

Without hesitation, she kissed him in return, abandoning any thoughts of denial. Everything inside her desired this moment, this man, his body inside her, joined together.

Snuggling as close as possible without actually passing through skin, she wrapped her arms around his neck and let her fingers do what they'd wanted to do for so long. Threading them through his hair, she arched her body to show her response and molded her breasts into his hard chest.

Within seconds, he'd pushed aside the table and lowered her until she lay on the soft rug fully under him. Her lips searched for his and they kissed again, their breathing harsh and intense.

"Stop me, baby. You're fragile. You need—"

"I need you. Oh, Danny, I need you."

No sooner had the words left her lips than he'd claimed them again. This time his kiss lit every nerve ending in her body, and she felt continuous explosions occur after multiple detonations.

Suddenly his body stiffened, and the shock made her hesitate.

"God... No!" He thrust her gently to the side and tried to roll away, but her arms wouldn't let go. Purposely, he faced the other way, hiding his eyes.

"Dan! Don't leave me like this."

"I'm a hard man, baby. I don't know how to be soft, to be the kind of person you deserve in your life. I've never had anyone, never wanted any..." His voice petered away as if the words couldn't be spoken. Then he ground out the phrase that almost made her earlier tears form again. "For me, Kandi, it won't be a one-night stand. If we continue, I'm hooked forever. If you can't stand the thought, then leave the room and we'll pretend this never happened."

"Oh, love, I'm not going anywhere." She spoke in his ear and then kissed his cheek, her lips taking their time.

Her words rang in the silence and he slowly

faced her, his intense eyes questioning, his mouth shut tight. If it weren't for the twitching in his left cheek, she might have thought him uncaring, and not have understood the toll this moment was taking on the precious man.

Emotion vibrated from every muscle of his body and she saw the façade crumble just before he sought her lips in a kiss that seared her to her very soul. When his chin trembled, love flooded into her heart uniting compassion with passion. His vulnerability gave her power, and it was time to give it back.

Chapter Forty-nine

Dan heard her whispered words and had to see for himself if she'd understood the gravity of his meaning. If this woman let him love her completely, he'd never be the same person again.

He'd kept her safe in his heart all these years, and to finally have the chance to be with the real, live woman and not just a fading memory would be the ultimate. If he lost her again, it would break him. He wasn't sure if he'd be able to go on.

Sensing her complete surrender, he let her show him by actions how much she wanted them to be together. Having her slide into his arms, wind herself around his body and push herself against him worked its magic. Her moans and whimpers of desire also helped. But the words she added, "I'm here," were all it took. Control snapped, and he scooped her even closer.

Hands trembling, he filtered his fingers through her beautiful hair and clutched her face for his kisses. Her mews of happiness spurred him on and he searched for her breasts, hating the clothes caught between them. When he reached under the nurse's scrubs, she quickly undid any hooks to give him full access to her lovely breasts.

A perfect handful, he fondled them gently until they drew his mouth. Licking and kissing her fleshy mounds made his body engorge past the point of comfort. It throbbed, and restraint became tenuous.

Not wanting to frighten her with his need, he slowed things down by pulling away and looking at her body. Seeing her writhe, sweat pooling on her chest, her hunger so openly revealed made a swirl of thankfulness and joy clutch at him. He kissed her deeply, with every bit of love he'd stored for years pouring from his lips.

"Danny, please. I need you." Passion shimmering like an aura around her, she reached for him, curved her body and thrust it toward him in invitation. Showed him in every way she could that he should take what she so lovingly offered.

A cry broke from him and he sank into her embrace, the last of his resistance gone. He'd take the chance that he meant something to her, that she wouldn't hurt him or leave him again. Truth be told, he had no choice.

Chapter Fifty

Greedy with hunger, spurring him on, Kandi moaned, "Please. Help me." She reached for the buttons on his shirt and then, losing all dexterity, she yanked at it, trying to bring the cloth out from under his belt. The need to touch his bare skin had become paramount and wouldn't be denied.

Realizing her intention, he began disrobing in between stealing more kisses and helping her to strip. As soon as she found his nakedness, all her attention became riveted on his body: the firm muscles in his arms and back, his lean hips and the rigid, male protrusion between his legs.

Drenched, ecstasy stimulating her beyond bearing, she loved when his fingers probed inside. His harsh moans of approval spurred her on and she thrust her hips forward in invitation.

He didn't respond quickly enough, and she couldn't take his tormenting tenderness any longer. Straddling him, she forced herself on top and impaled herself on the rigid proof of his desire.

"Kandi!" He stiffened. His pace changed immediately. Without losing his place, he lifted her as if she weighed nothing and flipped them back over so he lay on top. With rolling thrusts, her slick, tight body welcoming, he took her to heights she never thought possible.

Wild from her first-ever orgasm, she sobbed with pleasure and her drenched body pulsated and quivered its release. With one last thrust, shuddering, he poured himself into her, and all the while, his love words broke the silence.

"You love me?" After moments of recovery, she opened her eyes and found him gazing down at her, adoration coloring the usual black in his eyes with streaks of sparkling sapphire.

Stunned by the sight, she reached up and caressed the sides of his face. Her fingers smoothed the lines beside his brows, and then they traced the thickness of his lips that had given her such delight.

"Always. I've always loved you."

"You mean from the time we met."

"Yes." He smiled in a way that brought questions she wanted answered.

"Tell me."

While she pulled the throw blanket from the sofa over their cooling bodies, he reached to his pants and searched for his wallet. By the time, he'd straightened; she had two pillows behind them so they could lie side by side.

He pulled out a photograph that had obviously been well handled, that is if one took in the creases and discoloration from age into account.

Before he passed it over, he turned to her and propped his head on his hand so he could watch her reaction. Stunned, she looked first at his tender smile and then finally at the picture.

Recognition hit her immediately. "It's me."

"Yes."

Rearing back, she stared at his features, and a smile lit her heart.

"You're the boy on the bus."

Chapter
Fifty-one

"Yes." Too choked to talk, Dan nodded and then swallowed. Her delight had done it, turned him into a blithering idiot, and he needed to take a few breaths before totally making an ass out of himself.

"You left me. I remember, I was so worried about you disappearing. Truthfully, I missed you terribly."

Being bashed on the back of the head with a brick wouldn't have made as much of an impact as her soft confession.

"You did? Baby, I had no choice. My old man would have killed me if I'd stayed. But after I left, you didn't ride the bus anymore, right?" His searching gaze watched for her avowal, and he breathed a sigh of relief when she nodded.

"Right. From then on, my dad drove me every day. But how did you know?"

"Because I followed you home that last day and had a little talk with your father. I told him there were some creeps riding that bus and without me to watch over you, they'd give you a hard time. He promised he'd take care of it."

"He did. We had the biggest fight. I didn't want to stop seeing you, so I snuck onto the bus one day, but you didn't show up. He followed and was furious. Even though I argued, he wouldn't give in. He drove me to school after that until he'd made a bundle on one of his toys. Then he sent me to a private school where I lived on the campus all week. I loved it." She watched Dan's expression, and he sensed her question before she asked.

"What happened to you, Danny?"

"You understand... no one has ever called me that before. From you, I like it. Anyone else, they'd be in the hospital."

"Okay, I'll find another nickname. Quit changing the subject, hardass!"

"Nah! I like Danny better."

Her giggle made him laugh. Uncomfortable with sharing, he hedged, trying to decide how much she needed to know. As if she read his mind, she spoke gently but with a firmness he couldn't ignore. "Everything! I want to know everything."

"I might need some liquid courage before opening that Pandora's Box. Do you have any whiskey?"

She struggled out of his arms and rose, her pale, naked body beautiful in the light from the lamp they'd left on. With her blonde hair streaming down her back, her tiny waist highlighting the flare of her hips, the vision made him harden and his hunger returned in full force.

She didn't seem to be shy, and he liked that she trusted him. "I'll get us a picnic—whiskey for you and wine for me, with chips and dip. I love salty foods." As she sauntered into the kitchen to gather everything for their treat, he watched her flaunt her nakedness and could have sworn she added an extra wiggle before disappearing.

Lying there with his arm pillowing his head, he swallowed a lump the size of his fist. Glancing around the warm designer space, he gloried in the fact that he wasn't in his dreary hotel room or his own basic, cheerless home in Washington. Wanting to rise but knowing his knees would give out if he tried; Dan looked again at his picture... the one that had kept loneliness at bay for so many years.

She was here with him in person, a dream come true. He only prayed that after what he had to share, she wouldn't send him away.

Chapter
Fifty-two

Kandi hurried through to her bedroom so she could refresh herself and grab a filmy housecoat. Though she'd teasingly strutted her stuff in front of Dan, it wasn't something she'd normally do, and had no idea what had come over her to make her act like such a bimbo.

From the sound of him catching his breath and the groan that followed, she knew he'd appreciated her performance and the thought filled her with smug pleasure. The influence she had on this man scared her a little. He was so vulnerable, and she sensed she could hurt him... bad.

Therefore, whatever he had to confess, she'd better be open-minded, make no judgement. But then, wasn't that the way she lived her life?

Accepting people for who they were — no criticizing or condemning? People often commented it was that ability which made her so good at her job.

Carrying the tray into the living room, she saw he'd taken the time to refresh himself too, and that he now wore crumpled suit pants and an unbuttoned shirt. Usually immaculate, this dishevelment made him appear all the more endearing. She liked him like this. Especially his naked chest revealing a six-pack that made her heart quicken in anticipation.

"I saw you'd covered up and thought I should too." Nervousness, most likely an emotion he disliked or wasn't used to, made his voice crack. He swung away from her, one hand rubbing the back of his head and the other gripping his hip.

She set down the tray and poured him a glass half full of whiskey. When she took it to him, she purposely held out the glass and walked past his stretched arm to give him a hug. "Come." She took his free hand. "Sit down beside me. You talk. I'll listen. It'll be fine."

He followed her to the couch and tried to sit at one end alone, only she'd have none of that nonsense. "No! We're snuggling."

"Snuggling? Okay, fine. Show me." His laugh rang with relief and turned her insides to mush.

What in the world did this successful man have on his conscience? Worry suddenly seeped in, and she pushed it away. Dan had a good soul. She had no doubt. Years ago, hadn't he stepped in and saved her from a bad experience? And that had happened when he was only a boy.

Protecting someone weaker had come naturally. Strong, with a hardened core from having to do a difficult job—not easy and not possible for someone weak—he was a man to admire. Not fear.

Taking the initiative, she leaned over and kissed him. Softly, with affection, showing him he was safe. "Now, tell me."

And so, he did. Words poured from behind a tough shell that had kept him silent forever.

"The day I didn't show up, my stepdad had done a number on me. I knew you'd be frightened by my face. I couldn't do that to you, give you nightmares. So, instead I visited your dad and shocked the hell out of him. I let him believe I'd taken the beating on the bus and that scared the shit out of him. But he took me seriously about you never riding alone. He promised he'd make sure you were safe."

"Why?"

"Why what?"

"You're hedging. Why wouldn't you be riding the bus after you healed?"

"Because I had to leave." Dan sighed and gulped the whiskey. Leaning forward, he unwound his arm from behind her and used both hands to grip the glass. "My old man was a big guy, a lot stronger than me, and I'd always taken the beatings without even trying to fight back. But that morning, he lost it completely. He would have killed me. I knew if I didn't do something, he wouldn't stop. I had no choice but to protect myself, and I did."

Her heart faltered. "You killed him?"

He turned her way, his narrow-eyed gaze searching. "You're asking. Why?"

"You said he *was* a big guy."

Dan relaxed. "Right! I did. Actually, he shrunk a hell of a lot with the bone cancer that took him a few years ago."

Wishing she could feel sincere sympathy for the brute, she dug deep. *Nothing!* The only sadness in her heart was for Dan. "I'm sorry."

"No, in a way you're right. I thought I had killed him, Kandi. I wanted him to die, the bastard. He ate mean for breakfast and loved hurting anyone weaker. Up until then, I'd believed him to be my real father. And knowing I had his genes sickened me. When I thought I'd killed him, I knew I had to get away. I planned to run, but I couldn't leave you defenseless. That's why I went to see your dad."

"Even at a time like that, you thought about me? I always knew you cared. I used to make up daydreams about you."

Again, he swiveled her way, his expression totally shocked. "You did?" A smile seeped out and she reached to kiss his cheek right at the point where a small dimple appeared.

"Of course! You were my hero. I wanted to talk

to you, but you were so aloof that I lost my nerve every time. I thought you didn't want to be seen with a little girl like me. Back then, I was terribly shy, scared of my own shadow."

"You were the only person who mattered. I think I fell for you the first time you smiled at me, like I was important or something. Every day, I rushed to the bus so I could get to see you. You made me feel good about myself, and you were the only one. Talk about a boy's first crush."

"I used to look for you, too. And the days when you'd hide your face, I knew the night before had been terrible. I wanted so badly to tell you how sorry I was."

"He was a bastard, and I was the only one he could beat on. That last time, he really snapped. I had to defend myself."

"But, he didn't die, right?"

"No. But he ended up in the hospital for a few weeks. I learned then that we weren't actually related. He wanted me charged, and when one of the cops asked him why he'd want to charge his own kid, he ranted about how we weren't blood relatives. I was just a step-kid he'd kept after my mom had died."

"And so, you ran."

"Not exactly. After I talked to your father, I went to a Fed who lived in our building and gave myself up. He helped me. The cops stuck me in juvie until everything got sorted out. Once my old man turned the corner, they released me into this agent's custody. The guy, Bob Mires, was moving up in the bureau; his career had begun to take off. He'd lost his wife and lived a lonely existence until he took me under his wing."

"Bob Mires? The Director of FBI in Washington, Bob Mires?"

"That's him. Once he became involved, he got my sentence expunged, but only on the deal that he'd take responsibility for me. Keep me out of trouble and give me a home. I had no choice. That, or detention until I hit seventeen and a record to follow me for the rest of my life."

"You chose Mires."

"Yes. The only reason I hesitated at all was that they were transferring him to Washington and I'd have to go with him."

"And leave me."

He waved the photo. "I never left you."

Chapter Fifty-three

While Kandi slept in his arms, Dan laid beside her too happy to sleep. Instead, he thought back to the time when Bob had come to see him at the center. Bob had explained how he'd be prepared to put himself on the line if Dan would give him a chance.

Dan had gauged his sincerity and he remembered asking. "Why? Why are you willing to do what they say and take me on?" Even in those days, he'd had a bullshit meter that never failed him.

After Mires had explained his situation, about being a widower, needing someone to care for and having the wherewithal to make a difference, Dan had still asked, "Yeah, I get all that. But... why me?"

"Because you helped my wife. The day she'd

suffered her first stroke, she'd tripped on the stairs and you came along. She told me about how you'd helped her to the apartment, put the groceries away and wouldn't leave her until you saw me coming into the building."

Remembering the day, Dan admitted, "I wanted to call an ambulance but she wouldn't let me."

"Yeah, I know. She said you'd made her a deal. Either she called me or you'd go against her wishes."

"Man, she looked so sick. I couldn't just leave her there."

"It was because of you that she wasn't alone when she died. Once I got home, she told me about your kindness. How she wished she could have given me a son just like you. Someone who cared enough about another person to stop and help them, rather than ignoring what wasn't their business."

"I didn't know what to do."

"You did just fine. After I got home, we talked for some time before she'd finally allowed me to call the ambulance. On the way to the hospital, she suffered a cardiac arrest. But, I had that precious time with her because of what you did. I owe you for that...big time. So let me help you out of this mess. Let me send you to school, give you the chance at the kind of life you deserve."

Remembering how hard it had been not to break down, Dan still got emotional every time he thought about those moments when his life had changed forever.

Bob Mires had added, "There's just one thing you need to know."

Oh, oh! Here it comes. In his experience, there was always a snag...

"Yeah, whatever. There's always something."

"No, it's doable, Dan. They've just offered me a transfer to Washington to work in the bureau there. It's a position I've hoped for, and now that Miranda is gone, it's the best thing that could happen to me. I need to get away from this place, from the memories. Plus, the bureau has promised to make things happen for you to go to a school there. That is, if you want to."

A future! Something positive to consider. He'd thought back to the scorn Kandi's father hadn't hidden and how it had hurt worse than any punch from his prick of a step-dad. That man would never accept him around his little girl. And Dan didn't blame him at all.

An uncared for, scruffy, snot-nosed hoodlum, bloody and bruised by a scornful asshole who thankfully hadn't been his real dad, had no business thinking he could fit in.

Soul-searching over, Dan accepted his lack of choices. If he passed up this opportunity to change his life around, he'd never get another.

Suddenly, Kandi stirred. Her warm hands caressed his chest and she snuggled closer. They'd moved to her king-size bed, two people squeezed together, taking up very little space. Relaxing his tenseness, he let her soothe him.

"You're worried. Why?" Husky, her voice startled him and he quickly stroked her face, pushing the mass of curls behind her shoulder.

"Just thinking of the past. Once I opened that door, I can't seem to get it closed again."

Kandi leaned over him so her lips could soothe with kisses both gentle and inviting. "Don't close the door. Leave it open and let me in. I want to hear all about you. How you recognized me when you first arrived."

Dan stiffened and knew she'd sensed his discomfort.

She pulled back and he watched the wily woman come to the conclusion he'd never wanted her to reach.

Shit, shit, shit!

Chapter
Fifty-four

She wrenched herself out of his arms and Dan flinched. "You bastard! You knew all about me from the beginning. Where I worked and what I did."

He sat up with his back against the headboard and tried not to look too guilty. "Kandi, I had to know what had happened to you. That you were safe." Suddenly, he shifted his eyes away. "Then one day after I'd been with the agency for some time, curiosity got the better of me, and I did a background check."

"And found out I was an agent."

"Before then."

"When I was training at Quantico?"

"Yes."

"Were you Bob Mires' assistant then?"

"Not yet."

"So, you stalked me even then."

Stalked? He winced. *This wasn't going very well.* Satan's voice whispered in his head, warning him to leave, flee the danger and save his heart. He couldn't. If they had any chance for a future, it was past time to 'fess up. "In a manner of speaking."

"Bullshit. You were probably the reason I got all the shit jobs as a glorified office clerk."

Dan turned his face away and swallowed... hard. *"You didn't?"*

"I might have instigated some of the restrictions. You weren't the right person to be involved in homicide or with the drug—"

"Hey, I passed all the fitness tests, the oral and written exams with huge scores, and even excelled in the leadership roles."

"I know. But even you have to admit that being a crisis negotiator has worked out just perfectly. You've shone there."

"Only after I got hooked up with Bobbi and Wes. Before then, they held me back until I wanted to screa..." She stared at him and caught the twitch under his eyes. "You! It was your fault."

Shame-faced, Dan shuffled to the edge of the bed and would have bolted if she hadn't held his arm. Not wanting to shake her off or reject her in any way, he stalled and turned back to take his medicine like a man. Except that her naked breasts gleaming in the dim light from the hallway turned his thought processes to that of a gibbering idiot.

"No. I mean maybe. Some of it." He held up the blanket to cover her, which she pushed away. His moan probably satisfied the bitch in her. "But, in the end, you got what you wanted. They recognized your talent, and now you're chosen more than anyone else."

"Only because of a fluke."

"Excuse me?"

"One day, they'd sent me to interview a pending witness, and I came across another crime in progress."

"The Moore case—a woman who threatened to kill both her kids and herself."

"Yes. Bobbi and Wes had been called out and were getting nowhere. I couldn't help getting involved."

"You talked her down. The file recorded some of what happened, but I always wondered how you knew what to say."

"Simple. Mrs. Moore had had a meltdown because she couldn't afford her prescription drugs. She'd been taking half pills and had run out the day before. The poor woman felt like crap. Bobbi and Wes had been concentrating on making her see that she didn't really want to hurt her kids, that she'd always been such a good mother. But I knew the sick woman had blanked out on everything but her own suffering. It wasn't about them. It was always about her. The poor thing needed sympathy, someone who gave a damn that her life was so sad, so hard. Once I convinced her that I cared, she gave up the gun and exchanged it for a hug. She's fine now by the way. In case you care."

Fuck! "Of course, I care. She had a lot of support from the D.A., didn't she?"

***

"*You!*" Kandi didn't know whether to hit him over the head or kiss the man silly.

"It mattered to you. Therefore, it mattered to me."

"My job matters to me."

The frustrated growl he didn't try to hide soothed her just a bit. "Well... you got on their team, didn't you? Now you're in the middle of every crazy pile of shit that goes down in this city."

"Yes. Because I'm good at my job."

"*I know!*" He shouted his comeback, and the words echoed in the darkened room. Then he lowered his tone. "I know, Cupcake. Goddammit, no matter how hard I tried to protect you, things would happen, and you'd end up in the middle of one catastrophe after another."

She hated that he had his back to her. But she knew this was a critical moment in their future relationship. He had to understand. She was a qualified Special Agent with the Seattle branch of the Federal Bureau of Investigation, and no matter how much he hated that fact, she'd chosen it as her career.

"Wanna hear something even crazier?" He stiffened, obviously bracing himself for what was coming.

"I don't know, do I?"

"Uh, huh, you do. Look at me."

He did as she ordered and let her take his hand between both of hers.

"You need to know this part, Danny. The crazy thing about this whole situation is that you were instrumental in my choosing the FBI as a profession. The day you helped me on the bus, fought for me and saved me from that creep, I'd felt useless. More frightened than I'd ever felt before in my sheltered life. That incident made me aware that not everyone is kind or cares about others. If I could do something about that when I grew up, then I needed to. I wanted to be strong like you, be able to stick up for myself and yet still care about the underdog, their feelings and their problems."

His eyes widened with consternation. Yet she sensed the pride he couldn't hide. "Yeah?"

"God's truth."

"Hell, girl. From the time I began following your career, I've been proud of your accomplishments. No matter how terrified I was that you'd be injured, hurt by some crazed-out, sick dirt-bag, I've never stopped caring."

Silence seeped into the tension and made it swell. She stared at him and instantly recognized his vulnerability. Tears he fought hard appeared in his soulful eyes, and the jagged piercing doubts that had begun to cut up her insides vanished. She flung herself into his arms and smothered him with kisses.

A moan escaped as he swept her close, laid her down and followed. She knew exactly how to clear the air. Rubbing her nakedness against his in invitation, she kissed him silly.

At first, Blue's frantic barking didn't register. Caught up in the moment, with his hands gently caressing her breasts, his lips buried in the erotic zones between her head and shoulders, and his more sensitive member plunging deep into familiar territory, investigating Blue's uproar didn't rate high on her agenda.

But damn it if the barking didn't escalate...

Chapter
Fifty-five

Ben Warner continued glaring at the growling canine whose warnings were still being issued periodically. "Blasted animal wanted to eat me."

"And yet you're relatively unscathed." Kandi didn't try to hide her smile. "Dad, Blue's a guard dog and he didn't even bite you. Look, why are you prowling around at four o'clock in the morning? Wait, don't tell me. Your local certified stoolpigeons found out about the Dixon situation and blabbed to you."

"What are you talking about?" His hedging wasn't at all convincing.

"You know damn well. Quit playing the silly prick trick."

"Watch your trash talking, young lady, and the

tone you're taking with your poor old father." Ben's playacting earned him an even louder warning from a dog with no sense of humor.

Kandi laughed and went over to soothe her pet. Then she gave her dad a hug so her canine bodyguard would see Ben was a friend. "Don't get so riled. I'm just using your own pet expression back at you."

Slightly less peeved, Ben admitted, "I might have been informed about an incident where my baby girl was abducted by killers, lured on board a broken-down, dirty old trawler and had to fight for her life using a poisonous substance her brilliant dad had invented. It quite possibly prompted me to leave my bed and fly down here as fast as the helicopter pilot could make the flight." His quirky habit of blinking his eyelashes and wriggling his eyebrows made her giggle, like it had all her life.

"And Frick and Frack, your informants, were on the phone to you as soon as the word got out, right?"

"Well, hell, Kandice Warner. A dad needs to know what's happening in his little girl's life. Especially when she's chosen to be a modern-day, gun-toting agent. How was I to know you'd acquired a live-in, two-legged protector and this vicious brute as his sidekick?"

"Dan didn't punch you."

"Only because you screamed out in time. I saw his eyes and they were colder than Toby's arse."

"I always wanted to know who this Toby guy you constantly refer to is." She giggled and earned a black look from her dad.

"Quit trying to change the subject. That half-dressed human pile-driver came out of your house at four in the morning. Now, I'm just a mite concerned about that." He looked at her, but she ignored his questioning stare.

Instead, she looked over to see that Dan was still on the phone, calling off the back-up he'd arranged when they'd first heard Blue barking. Finished, he joined them at the kitchen counter and picked up the mug of coffee she'd placed there for him.

Knowing her dad didn't appreciate Dan's undressed, rumpled appearance as much as she did, she had to admit that, without his normal authoritative demeanor and his slightly cold mask, Dan appeared more endearing.

Apprehension rode him, and though he tried to hide his uneasiness she sensed it clearly. When he looked at her dad, as if she were still a little girl and he a hard-rock kid, a worried frown appeared.

"I'm sorry I attacked you, sir, but I couldn't see what you were holding and because of recent ah... events, I wasn't about to chance that it could be a weapon."

"So what you're saying is I'm freakin' lucky you weren't carrying a gun or you'd have shot me for brandishing an iPhone."

Spotting Kandi's wink, Dan's harshness eased

off and he replied, "Nah! Instead of shooting you, I'd have just given Blue the go-ahead."

Kandi knew her laughter put the sour look on her dad's face but he deserved to take some responsibility in this craziness. "Dad, come on. You build me a house like a fortified modern stockade, and then you sneak in and override those same safety features when you want to invade my privacy. What's that all about, huh? If it weren't for Blue, you'd have been able to enter and we'd never have known you were here."

Looking sheepish, turning to Dan for support and finding nothing but a raised eyebrow and a man waiting for answers, Ben huffed his resentment. "Okay, already. I thought I'd just check in on you like I used to when you were still my little girl." Ben watched for Kandi's usual softening, but she held firm. So he added more soft-soaping. "And I'd be here to cook your favorite specialty breakfast. The one you always loved."

"Oh, great chef, you mean Pop Tarts?"

"Yes! The strawberry ones."

"Dad, from the time I found out that *real* strawberries were a lot tastier, I never liked them. You liked them and I ate them to please you."

"Okay, now you're breakin' my heart, kiddo."

Laughing like she always did at his foolishness, never being able to stay mad at the man who so obviously loved her, she hugged him again, and her heart sang when, from the corner of her eye, she saw him wink at Dan and watched her lover grin in return.

***

Dan knew Ben Warner had caught on that he'd been in Kandi's bed earlier and blatantly returning there would have been just too awkward. Especially, when one day soon, he wanted this man as his ally so he could marry his daughter.

Kandi followed him into her bedroom and her luring smile almost convinced him to stay. But the sun would soon be up and he had a busy day ahead. "Quit tempting me, you little witch."

"We still have a couple of hours before we need to be at the office."

"You mean, *I* have to be at the office. You're officially on leave until next week."

She stiffened. "Why? That's not fair. I'm fine."

"You're exhausted. And I should be shot for taking advantage of you in your weakened condition."

She approached and slid her arms inside his suit jacket. "I remember it the other way around. You were going to leave me and I wouldn't let you." She kissed the under part of his chin and nibbled her way to his lips.

He kissed her, his lips demanding a response. Then, before they could get carried away, he held her in place while he stepped back. "Stop it, brat. You know you're impossible to resist"

"And yet, you're doing so."

"Right. And it's damned hard."

She grinned. "I know. Makes me feel all-powerful."

He laughed at her crowing and kissed her again. "You're *still* on leave."

Stung, she crossed her arms and pouted. "I have all the paperwork to catch up on, and there'll be an inquiry."

"Fine, fill them in at home and e-mail them to me. I'll have Wes call you if we need you in person. In the meantime, visit with Bobbi at the hospital and behave. I'll call you for dinner... tonight?"

"Can't. I'm busy." She waited to see if he'd rise to her ploy but he just nodded.

Unable to stand his pretence of not being hurt, she broke down. "Wes and Patti invited a bunch of us to share in some good news and we're all meeting at the Kingdom Steakhouse downtown. Would you like to come as my date?"

A bell rang in his conscience and stopped him from replying quickly. She caught his hesitation and surprised him with her insight.

Speaking with intent, needing an answer, she asked, "Either you don't want to be seen dating me because of stupid bureau policies, or, even after everything we've been through, you still believe that Wes is dirty. Which is it?"

"What time should I pick you up?"

Chapter
Fifty-six

Kandi used her day to catch up on all kinds of chores. But first, she'd grabbed a few hours more sleep and then breakfast with her dad. Bookwork had taken up another chunk of time, and then finally she was heading down the hospital corridor.

Having checked in first with Mrs. Kravitz and found out the good news that the woman would pull through and that the D.A. and the Mayor were working out a deal for Bernie's sentence, it was hard to wipe the smile off her face or settle the bounce in her steps. Happy now, she started toward Bobbi's room.

Feeling on top of the world, her memories from the night spent with Danny snuck in and warmth invaded every area of her body. She smiled at everyone she met.

Noise up ahead warned her of a problem. Before she rounded the corridor and saw the bleak situation for herself, she took a deep breath and composed herself. Intuition kicked in that she'd need to keep her wits about her. But burned out from the previous stresses, this time it wouldn't be easy.

Nurses were crowded together behind the work station and a few doctors were huddled against a back wall. Two police officers, Harvey Cruiz and his partner, along with a hospital security guard, one with a gash in his arm, had cornered the patient. The distraught man had a female doctor held prisoner with his arm around her throat and a pair of sharp scissors to her cheek.

Because of his shaking, he'd pierced her skin and Kandi saw the blood seeping. Mixing with the tears washing in rivulets down her face, this image made the scene more horrific than it would have been. She also saw the panic in the woman's eyes, her trembling lips and her weakening knees. Mostly the strength of her abductor was what kept her upright.

Quickly, producing her ID, Kandi stepped forward and pushed one of the nurse's rolling office chairs in front of her. When she knew the crazy had seen her—that she had his complete attention—she waited for him to erupt and wasn't disappointed.

"You, crazy woman, stop right there. Another step and I'll kill her." The middle-aged man's hard voice held conviction and his words, though harsh, weren't slurred.

His wild black hair and unshaven face distracted from the fact that his one eye was swollen and there were cuts and bruises on his face. Otherwise, he seemed clear-headed, not a homeless alcoholic or someone on drugs.

Relieved to see she wasn't dealing with a crazy who was completely out of control, Kandi followed directions and stopped. She slowly took her seat on the chair, crossed her legs and made herself comfortable. Knowing the perp hadn't taken his eyes off her, and that she'd thrown him as planned, she smiled pleasantly. "I'm Special Agent, Kandice Warner with the Seattle Bureau of Investigations. You seem upset, sir."

He scanned at the others waiting to pounce and snarled, "You think? I got me a hostage, a weapon and a reason to kill. One might presume to believe there's a problem."

"Exactly what I thought." Kandi beamed at him. "I know you won't let go of the poor doctor, but you might like to release the pressure just a little, or she'll pass out and won't do you any good at all when these officers make their move."

Eyes narrowed, he glanced at the whimpering woman who he held. Kandi saw the doctor take a big breath and knew he'd followed her order. She'd also realized that he wasn't heartless. In fact, he'd whitened when he'd heard her comment, and she sensed his sorrow for hurting his prisoner.

Something's not as it seems... "Thank you. So maybe you can tell me why you're taking this extreme action. And, please, don't tell me you didn't like the Jell-o?" She grinned and was relieved to see his expression lighten. She even heard the snickers in the background and felt the tension easing all around.

The security fellow and the officers now turned to her, but she waved them back, wanting the offender to feel less threatened. Once he'd registered that she had taken charge, she leaned forward, hands clasped between her knees and said, "Now, sir, what can we do for you?"

"You mean it?"

"Oh, yeah! It's my job to make sure this situation is settled without anyone getting injured, and that includes you. So, tell me. What can we do to make this all go away?"

"Don't let them force me back to Tijuana until I do what I came here to do."

"And that is?"

"To save my little girl. She lives here in Seattle and she's dying. Her mama moved here with her a few years ago. My baby, Maria, has congenital nephrotic syndrome and the medicines aren't working anymore. She needs a kidney and I know I'm a match. But these bastards," he pointed at the officers, "are going to throw me out of the country. They caught me at the airport, beat the shit out of me so I needed treatment, and now they're going to send me back. They won't believe that I don't want to *stay* in your stinkin' country. All I want is to help save my daughter's life. Then I'll gladly leave."

"I see. While this ah... *stinkin'* country has the equipment, the knowledge and means to save your daughter's life, it's not that we don't want you here, it's just that we have proper channels."

"There was no time to go through your *proper channels*. Do you know how difficult it is, all that red tape and the bureaucratic bullshit that goes on? Meantime, my baby dies."

Kandi noticed a bystander holding her phone up, no doubt taking a video of the proceedings. Storing the identity of the woman, knowing she'd need that film before the day was over, Kandi let the man rant his fury until he seemed to have emptied himself.

"So, you tried sneaking in with a fake identity and were stopped. No doubt when they pulled you over, rather than discuss the situation rationally, you tried to fight your way out."

"No! I did everything I could to talk to them. Christ, I even fell on my knees and begged. No one would listen. Don't you get it? If they send me back, a little girl dies for no good reason. I offered to pay for the procedure. I'm not a rich man, but our village would be willing to help. We could make payments. I'd sell everything I own." By now, tears were dripping onto the doctor's hair and she was patting the loosened arm around her neck. "Here's her photo." He let go of his hostage long enough to reach into his pocket and pass the picture to the doctor who held it up.

Kandi, along with most in the area, leaned forward to see the smiling face of a pretty pre-schooler. Her long black curls flaunted a pink satin bow and she wore a huge smile.

The doctor, now loose, never moved away. Instead, she stood by her patient as if playing a part. *Could she be part of the crusade?*

Heart softened by the father's plea, Kandi replied, "Your Maria is beautiful. And, no, we can't let her die. So, what I suggest is we all settle down. I'll call the Mayor and we'll see what can be done. The people in Seattle are kind-hearted and there's no way they'd want your beautiful little girl to suffer from—what did you call it—bureaucratic bullshit. If they can organize the operation to be done here..." Kandi saw the doc's emphatic nod and hoped the camera picked it up. "Then maybe, just maybe, we can help you, Mr...?"

Wiping his face on his sleeve, the scissors no longer a threat, his sobbing reply made her swallow to stop the pity from escaping down her own cheeks. "My name is Romanis. Estevan Romanis. And you, lady, are the angel from my prayers."

"We'll get this straightened out, Estevan. I'm

betting the Mayor is on his way here as we speak."
She saw Harvey nod and knew the situation had
been monitored and her suggestion would be acted
on. She could always count on Harvey.

A slight ruckus occurred to Kandi's left and she
glanced over to see Officer Chris Radcock, a shoot-
'em-first-and ask-questions-later idiot, sneaking
onto the scene with his gun in his hand. The
scrawny cop had gotten on her bad side more times
than she wanted to count. Lucky for him, he had
an uncle on the force, one in a high position who
could pull strings.

Radcock, the stupid bastard, had a tiny, damaged
brain and a huge need to shine every opportunity
he could get.

Stiffening from intuition and a bad feeling, her
nerves jangled while silent screams of frustration
turned her fury red-hot. *What the hell is that jackass
doing here? And why in God's name does the fool have
his weapon drawn?*

Chapter
Fifty-seven

Not wanting to lose the momentum she'd painstakingly built so far, Kandi frowned at the jerk and saw his eyes widen. Then he shook his head and crept even closer, almost to the point where his gun would be visible.

"Estevan, excuse me for just a second and stay calm no matter what happens... for Maria."

He nodded, a question lighting his face.

Moving swiftly from a sitting pose to a flying leap, Kandi had the skinny asshole back up the hallway, away from the crowd and against the wall, in a second. A hard karate chop across his wrist made him drop his gun and her arm choking him against the wall made him stop struggling. "Are you crazy, Radcock? The situation is under control, and you showing up like Dirty Harry, pointing that ridiculous weapon that's almost as big as you are, would totally undo everything. Now beat it, or this time I swear, I'll have your badge."

"Hey, Agent Bitch, you can't do this. I'm on the job."

Harvey, who'd managed to sneak around the nurses' station and come out the other side, spoke up. "Do what she says, Chris. We don't want any trouble here."

Another voice broke into the discussion and settled the matter instantly. When ASAC Dan Black spoke, people tended to listen.

"Back off, Radcock, or *I'll* make sure that badge you're wearing disappears before the end of your shift."

Dan! Shooting him a grin and seeing him shaking his head as if to say, *Can't I ever let you out of my sight*, Kandi dropped her arm and returned to her chair.

"Sorry about that, Estevan. Everything's under control now. Do you trust me?"

"Yes. I do."

"Will you let the officers take you back to your room now?" She watched him look at the doctor, who was no longer his hostage, but who hadn't left his side, and she added, "With the doctor if you must, and I'll have the Mayor see you there."

Estevan glanced toward the doctor and as soon as she nodded, he spoke, "I'll do whatever you say, as long as I know you'll help me and Maria."

"I'll do everything I can."

"Agent Warner, you are a legend. I, and my family, thank you."

"Don't thank me yet. Let's see if we can get the surgeon to agree to perform the operation."

The hostage, his doctor, answered for him. "She agrees, Agent Warner. I'd like nothing better that to save Maria's life."

While two of the officers escorted Estevan, now handcuffed, back to his room, the scissors taken into police custody, Harvey soon had the crowd dispersed and the corridor cleared.

Kandi, motioning for Dan to wait, made a beeline to the witness with the phone still clutched in her hands. The satisfied smile animating her expression instantly disappeared when Kandi stopped her from entering the elevator.

"A moment please, ma'am. You filmed what happened today, right?"

Dressed haphazardly in cheap clothes, clutching a shoddy handbag, her hair frizzed around her face, the photographer stopped. "I hope I got it all. What a break. Do you mind if I take it to the local television station and get what I can for it? I could sure use the money with my husband laid up."

"What if I tell you I can get you a better deal? If you'll wait for a few minutes until the Mayor arrives and has a chance to get briefed, he'll most likely be dealing with Mr. Romanis. Not one to miss out on an opportunity like this, Mayor Wells will have his own cameraman with him, but they won't have the footage you do. Bet they'd be interested."

"That would be wonderful, Agent Warner. And can I just say—you were fantastic with that poor man. Everyone believed you really cared about him because you did. I've seen you a number of times on television helping others, and I'm thrilled to meet you in person and actually see you in action."

Uncomfortable, Kandi caught Harvey's eye and waved him over. "Just doing my job. But thanks for the kind words." Kandi patted her hand and loved the smile that lit up the woman's tired face. *Poor lady! Everyone has their problems.* "Officer Harvey here will show you where to wait until we're ready."

Dan had stood by, watching everything closely. As soon as Kandi was free, he came closer. "You seem to always know what to say to people. How the hell do you do that?"

"It's what I was trained for."

"Nah! It's not something you can learn, it's natural, inherited. You had that ability as a little girl. It's what made me your slave then."

"How about now?" The words came out throaty. Her voice had lowered — her intensity apparent. She moved closer, so their bodies barely touched. But it was enough for the lightning to sizzle and desires to burst free. Her hand snaked into his and she loved that he squeezed her fingers before letting her go.

The elevator doors opened, and an entourage spilled forward. Suddenly, the space became crowded. "Hello again, Agent Black." The Mayor shook hands with Dan, his respect obvious. "Agent Warner. We meet again in such a short time. I'm thrilled." His tone gave a different impression.

"Sure you are, Bob. I bet your gut tightened when you heard about this situation."

"It did when you summoned me to appear and deal with it personally."

"Hey, the people of Seattle love you and trust you'll do the right thing."

"Quit soft-soaping me, Kandi. You frost my ass, missy, and if I didn't like you so much, I'd get you fired. Have you any idea what kind of a shit-pool you've landed me in?"

"Yeah. I kinda do. Re-election's coming up soon, and after what happened on the roof with Kravitz your polling numbers are down. This story is a heartbreaker for anyone with a conscience and can make you look pretty sweet if you work it right."

All ears, Mayor Bob Wells directed a heated stare her way that would fry a lesser soul, and she didn't even flinch. Instead her eyebrows lifted, and she grinned engagingly. "Mayor, we got everything that happened on tape. The confession, Romanis getting beaten for fighting for his daughter's life, it's perfect. Don't worry, your people followed the book and did their jobs. They stopped an illegal at the airport. And Mr. Romanis, a father fighting to save his little girl, did his job. Everyone looks good. Now you need to step up and look good too."

"And how am I supposed to do that?"

"Make the deal. Let Maria have the operation, arrange for Mr. Romanis to pay for it and then ship him back. Hell, I'll kick in the first ten thousand, and no doubt my dad will add his donation. Let the folks who watch see if their hearts are in the right place too. Show the country that the Mayor and his followers here in Seattle have integrity, care about even their younger citizens and are willing to save a little girl's life. It's a win-win for you."

Nodding all the while he listened, she watched Mayor Wells' face lighten and a smile finally appear. "So, where's this tape..." Before he went to deal, he hugged her. "Thanks, Kandicane." Then he headed for the room where cameras would soon be rolling.

***

With his arm behind her back guiding her to the corner, Dan stepped into her space and glared teasingly. "Every time I let you out of my sight, you're in the middle of another incident."

"How did you find out about this and get here so fast?" Her questioning stare searched his eyes, but he played it cool.

"Not telling."

"You got spies following me, Danny?"

"My lips are sealed." He grinned and hoped she wouldn't pursue the subject.

"I can't imagine that they'd be good enough to fool me, but if you do, you'd better call off your dogs... well, all except Blue, of course." A grin broke loose, and she tried to look harsh but failed. "I don't appreciate being tailed or spied on."

"Okay, settle down. I was on my way to check on Agent Carter when I heard about the disturbance. But I'm beginning to think a bodyguard might not be such a bad idea."

A sassy look appeared. On tiptoe, she leaned in and quickly kissed his lips. "There's only one bodyguard I'd be happy with. Wanna apply for the position?"

His lips closing in on hers, Dan whispered, "You're a silver-tongued little devil, and I can't wait to have it in my mouth so I can taste just how sweet it is."

"That does it. Let's go home." She whirled, pushed against him and started shoving backwards.

Laughing, he stopped her, circled her face with his hands and tilted it so he could see her expression. Sparkling with humor, her passionate expression dug holes into his resolve and almost had him saying the hell with everything. "What about tonight with Wes and Patti? Their news? Are you willing to let them down?" Having a pretty good idea of what they were going to share, Dan knew that Kandi would be happy for her friends and should be there.

Her head lowered to his chest and she whispered. "You're a tease. Tempting me and then reminding me why it isn't possible."

God knows he wanted to sweep her up, get her in his car and head to her place to continue what they'd begun the night before. But he couldn't. There was a lot more at stake than a night out with Kandi.

Chapter
Fifty-eight

Hesitating at the door, Dan hoped the others at the restaurant didn't know how difficult this was for him. Normally, he could hold his own at almost any social function. After all, he'd spent a few years in the role of Assistant Director and was asked to appear often at different gatherings.

But rather than easing into the relaxed, yet distant persona he usually assumed, his palms were sweaty and the nerves under his eye had already begun their annoying spasms. Thank goodness, most people never noticed. Unless one looked close, he'd cover up and pretend a nonchalance he didn't feel.

Kandi searched his expression. "Do you want to go in or not? They're expecting me, and I know

Wes mentioned it to you 'cause he phoned and asked me if I thought you'd come. I told him he should at least give you an invitation."

Dan glanced through the front window of the brick building and watched the swelled crowd standing around, everyone laughing, joking, good feelings abounding. The white-linen covered tables held an array of tasty morsels and the folks were digging in, being sociable, having fun.

Soft light spilled onto the sidewalk where they stood, arms entwined, her head against his shoulder. "Don't tell me you're nervous. The big, tough, bureau hotshot scared of a small gathering of workers and friends." Her teasing hit home, but not in the way she'd intended.

His fear was more about her discovering a corrupt agent. And knowing how it would break her soft heart, the thought scared the bejesus out of him. The sting they'd set up would happen. It had to. Didn't mean he'd enjoy it.

"Yeah, Wes invited me. But I left it up in the air, told him the workload had doubled with the Dixons' mess, but I would try and check in for a little while."

He watched her thought processes at work. She stiffened and drew away. "Did you want us to pretend we met at the door?"

He glared at her, his attitude a lot harsher than he meant it to be. "Would you mind?"

"Would you ask?" She came right back at him.

"Not a chance. You're my date, and I'm proud to let the others see us together. Thank goodness, the FBI doesn't have strict rules against fraternization. But I guess if they did, we'd have to break them."

The smile that lit up her face almost put him on his ass. His knees started to give out and he had to hold onto her in a sly way so she wouldn't realize his dilemma. With both hands on her upper arms, he questioned. "Do you know who all's coming tonight?"

Beaming with happiness, she replied, "Wes just mentioned some family and a few personal friends from his orphanage days. His wife is a high school teacher and they may have added in her work associates too." She glanced in through the window. "I miss Bobbi. She wanted so badly to be here, but the doctor hadn't done his rounds yet and she couldn't get anyone to sign her discharge form. I'm just glad her sister is looking after Randy, her five-year-old son."

"I guess families do come in handy sometimes." He didn't mean to be disagreeable. The words hung in the air between them. He studied her reaction, and her soft smile had him breathing a sigh of relief.

"When a person is fortunate in their relatives, it can make life a lot more special. Maybe one day, you'll learn that's true."

Not sure what she was getting at, and too shy to delve, Dan switched topics. "Anyway, Bobbi sure bounced back. The woman's amazing. "

"Yes, she is. She's my family, her and Wes."

He swallowed and took the hit, though she hadn't meant to make things worse. "Okay, are you ready to face the music?"

"Lead on, boss man."

"Insubordinate little monkey." He kissed her forehead, opened the door and guided her forward. The first person he noticed—handsome and wearing designer clothes that cost a fortune—was the very man he'd come here to find.

Okay, asshole, let the games begin.

Chapter
Fifty-nine

Everyone clustered in groups, moving from one bunch to the other, visiting, being introduced and sharing like strangers tend to do at social functions such as tonight.

Almost as soon as they walked in, Kandi got separated from Dan. Patti, Wes's wife, took her arm and led her to the corner.

"Kandi, Wes told me a little of what you've been through since the last time we saw each other, and I just had to tell you how sorry I am. Personally, I don't know how you can go through days like you do and stay sane."

Rolling her eyes weirdly and twitching her head, Kandi joked. "Who's the liar that said I'm sane?"

Giggling, her tight red curls bouncing in the way

they did when she laughed, Patti hugged her. "Stop goofing around. You know how much Wes and I adore you. Please be careful out there." Her face turned serious, unlike her usual expression, and she added. "I have a premonition of bad times, my friend, and the feelings are stronger now that we're together. I want you to be extra cautious. I've warned Wes too, but he just poo-poos me and teases. Says it's because of the baby."

"Baby? Oh my God, that's what we're celebrating. You're pregnant!" Everything forgotten but the wonderful news, Kandi swept her friend into a huge hug, swaying back and forth with exuberance. "You're going to have a baby. No wonder Wes has been wearing a goofy grin lately, and... acting kinda forgetful. Wow! I'm ecstatic – for both of you." Kandi waved her hand slightly in front of Patti's stomach; a smile lighting up her insides, which she knew had to be splashed over her features. "Congratulations."

A seductive male voice interrupted. "So that's why there's a royal command for this dinner, *estás embarazada de mi amiga?* I'm thrilled at your news." George Lewis, Wes's best friend from their orphanage days, stepped closer and put his arm around Patti. "I couldn't be more delighted. You two deserve to be parents more than anyone else I know. Your kid will be a very fortunate child." He turned to Kandi and, as was his custom, bent to kiss her cheek. He raised his eyebrow when, right after, she put distance between them in a way as not to be rude... but damned close.

"Hi, George. It's nice you could be here tonight to share Wes and Patti's news."

"I wouldn't miss the chance to spend time with my good friends and see you again, *cariña*."

Kandi felt the frost gather that always did whenever she spent time in this man's company. Slithering squeamishness had started at her neck, attacked her back and moved over the rest of her body. After her recent talk with Dan about the FBI's suspicions, acting normal became even more difficult.

Playing a part, never an easy feat for Kandi, slipped into place and she behaved the same way in his company as she'd always done. Indifferent, friendly like one would be with a stranger, but keeping him at arm's length.

And in the same manner he always used, he came after her like a wolf scenting a female in heat. "Aw, Kandi, you get lovelier every time I see you." Before she could stop him, he touched her cheek gently in a caressing way that made her want to punch him for taking liberties. "You've been hurt. The bruise is barely noticeable, but I can see it. You tell me what bastard did this to you, and I'll teach him a lesson he won't soon forget."

"You put your hands on her again, and I'll teach *you* a lesson you won't soon forget." Dan stepped up behind her and, with his arm around her waist, brought her snug to his side. His grin belied the threat to anyone overhearing the words but the hard gleam in his eyes that connected to George said it all. *She's mine. Fuck off!*

George's greasy smile faltered for just a few seconds. But he recovered quickly. "Message received, *mi amigo*. I'm George Lewis, Wes's *amigo* from way back. And you are...?"

"Dan Black, Wes's colleague. I recently moved here from Washington."

"Ah! Yes. Wes told me his agency was getting a new Assistant to the Special Agent in Charge. That must be you."

"Guilty." Dan's voice had smoothed out to become impersonal.

Before they could carry on any further, across the room, Wes clanged a spoon against his glass. "The dining room is ready for us to go in and take our seats now."

In no time, everyone was seated at the long table that had been organized. George had maneuvered his way into sitting next to Wes at the head of the table, and Dan had led Kandi to the chair beside Patti, who of course, sat at Wes's right hand side.

Enjoying the wonderful mood of their hosts, the diners all laughed, and the jokes flew freely. Once the drinks were served and the meal followed, the guests dug in.

But knowing now that George was under investigation, and that the Bureau had doubts about Wes, Kandi ate sparingly, while paying more attention to the interaction between the two male orphanage friends than she'd ever done before.

Wes had laid his phone on the table as was his habit. *Hold it! Why the sneaky son-of-a-bitch!* Watching every move without appearing to do so, she saw when George made the switch. His own phone, the exact replica of Wes's, right down to the gimmicky cover Wes used, appeared for a split second and replaced the one on the table. Slick, like a trained magician, George had swapped phones.

Quickly, Kandi studied Wes. Snuggling with Patti, he'd turned his back to George. Anyone who didn't know him as well as Kandi did wouldn't have seen the slight stiffening of his body when the exchange took place. Though he never missed a beat teasing his wife, Kandi was positive he knew what George had done.

Her heart dropped!

Literally.

Sickening sensations twisted her insides. Agony ripped at her chest, making it hard for her to breathe. Fighting to hold on to her convictions, she searched her friend's expression and saw the innocence... yeah, but of an actor.

Oh, Wes!

Appalled, she turned to Dan expecting that he would have seen what had transpired, but the partner seated on his other side seemed to be keeping him amused. If the silly giggling from Patti's teacher friend was any indication, she'd breached Dan's aloof perimeters and was enjoying his attention.

And that seemed peculiar too. Why in the world had that leopard changed his spots at a time like this?

Questions rioted around in her skull until she felt like screaming. *What the hell is going on?* A disturbance at the entrance to their area caught everyone's attention, and suddenly Bobbi appeared.

Like an angel who'd received a message, her eyes caught Kandi's and she nodded knowingly, sensing, understanding that Kandi needed her close.

Taking charge, like only Bobbi could do, she directed the waitress to place an extra chair between Patti and Kandi's. "I want to be close to Patti. Put me next to her. Wes, you asshole, thanks for giving up on me. I told you I'd make it, come hell or high water."

Wes roared with laughter, a bit over the top. "I truly didn't believe you'd talk that doctor into letting you go. Even the nurse didn't think you'd be ready to leave for a few more days."

"What the hell do they know? I got home in time to give Randy his bath, read him a story and put him to bed. Then I changed and here I am, ready to celebrate whatever the hell news you've been holding out on from your partners. No doubt, the same news that's put that stupid smirk on your face lately."

Beaming, Wes looked to Patti for permission. Once she nodded, he took her hand and they both stood to make their announcement and receive everyone's good wishes.

By the time the guests had settled back down and returned to their seats, Kandi had control of herself. Once the waitress had taken Bobbi's order, and her partner had finished congratulating Patti, she leaned over to her left. "Yo, Cupcake. What's up? And why the hell are you paler than this fucking white tablecloth?"

Chapter Sixty

Meeting in the ladies' room after the meal that Kandi had either nibbled at or rearranged on her plate, she withstood her friend's barrage of questions. "I don't know what you mean."

"Looky-here, missy. Earlier today, you were floating on a cloud, all soft-faced and hearts beaming in your eyes. A mere few hours later, I find you looking like you'd lost your best friend. Something has to have happened, and I want to know what it is. What're you not telling me?"

Knowing that Dan had shared the bureau's suspicions with her in confidence, Kandi couldn't, with all good conscience, pass on the information to Bobbi without his consent. He was still her superior, and she had to respect his position.

"I can't tell you. Not because I don't want to. But I can't."

"Okay, what if I guess?"

"What do you mean?"

"Well, what if I say that I think Georgie-porgie has pissed you off in some way. Will you agree?"

Stunned, Kandi turned to Bobbi and held her stare, the one that was digging holes in her wall of resistance. "How the hell did you connect my attitude with George Lewis?"

"I stood at the doorway before making my entrance and I caught the stunned way you looked at him. Lordy, girl, disapproval dripped from those big — normally sparkling — blue eyes. If looks could kill..." Bobbi sliced at her neck with an imaginary knife. "You know what I'm sayin' here?"

"Shit! Do you think he noticed?"

"Nope. He was too busy looking innocently at the other end of the table. And I've told you before about that language. Whenever you use it, I know something's up. So, share. I'm your partner, aren't I?"

"Can't. Not because I don't want to. But because I'm under orders." Kandi smoothed her hand down Bobbi's arm. "Did you bring your car?"

"Of course, why?"

"I need it. I came with Dan. If things turn out the way I figure, I might have to take yours. Okay?"

"Sure, but I come with it. And before you argue, that's the deal."

"Fine. If George leaves early, come up with an excuse that we need to go too... maybe a problem with Randy."

When Bobbi looked as if she'd take it further, Kandi stopped her by holding up her hand. "And don't ask why."

"Honey, I'm full of good excuses. Just leave it to me."

Chapter
Sixty-one

While everyone began breaking up for the night, Kandi led Dan into the darkened hallway. "Dan, can I talk to you?" His arms opened, and she melted into his embrace. The kiss he branded her mouth with had her gasping for air and wanting more, a lot more.

"I've wanted to do that all night." He kissed her again.

Thoughts scattered, her mind shut down and her senses became engrossed in the delights of his soft mouth. The fullness of his lips created a haven she could lose herself in. The scent of his oft-used manly products filled her senses. *Dan! Hers!* She hated reverting back to reality.

Noises from interlopers coming close made her

break loose and stutter, "B-bobbi just got a call from her babysitter. Randy isn't well. I should go home with her, just in case."

"Sure, I'll drive you." He gathered her face and, both hands delving into the soft curls hanging over her shoulders, he placed a sweet kiss on her forehead.

She put her hands against his chest, loving the hard muscles that she knew were hidden by his light grey suit jacket. "No, I'll just go with her and probably stay the night in case it's serious. You know kids and how they can be deathly ill with a high temperature one minute and fine the next."

"Not really, but I'll take your word for it." He grinned and leaned his forehead against hers, his hands stroking the nakedness of her back." Did I tell you how much I like this deceptive little black dress you're wearing?"

"Bet you like the back better than the front." She grinned and caught his answering smile.

"Too much material on this side." He slid his hands lightly over her chest, gliding softly over her breasts.

"And there's not enough on the other."

"Oh, I hadn't noticed." He chuckled softly. His hands stroked the bare skin of her back to just above the waistline.

"She's waiting for me, Danny. Let me go." Though she said the words, she didn't step away.

"Does that mean I have to sleep in my own bed

tonight?"

"If all is well, I'll call you. But if it's too late, I'll take a rain check for tomorrow."

Grumbling, he agreed and let her go. "Okay. I understand. But I'll keep my phone close."

***

Now, riding in the car, following George Lewis in his, Kandi felt Bobbi staring at her. "Just don't lose him. I want to know where he's going."

"No problem. The idiot isn't suspecting that two FBI agents are tailing him — for reasons known to only one of said agents." Disgust throbbed in Bobbi's voice and made Kandi wince.

"There's rumors he's involved with one of the gangs here in town. Running drugs maybe. I just needed to see where he hangs out."

"And you don't think that two chicks all dolled up in short dresses, stiletto heels and made up for an evening on the town might stick out like two sore thumbs in a cheap hole in the wall like the ones in this neighborhood?"

Kandi laughed. "Never thought of that. Let's just wait and see where he goes." Gladness filled her, mostly relief from being alone with Bobbi like old times. "Watch, he's turning south there."

"I see him. I'm on it, but I can't follow too close or he'll tag us. I think he's pulling into that parking arcade. What do you want me to do?"

"The wily bastard! I wonder if he knows he's being followed."

"I'm going to swing around and park further up the street. We can watch and wait for him to leave from there."

"Slow down here. He's stopped and giving over his keys. He's walking back to the street. Bet he's headed for the joint across there. I've heard of that nightclub."

"Me too. Actually, it's swankier than it looks from the outside. And... it's the perfect hangout for anyone who wants to keep a low profile."

"How do you know?" Kandi's surprise sounded in her voice.

"Remember, I was there about a year ago, undercover on the Weston case. You know the one about the high-class prostitutes?"

"I only remember that when you found out how much they were making, I had to talk you down." Kandi giggled. Bobbi had listed numerous pros to becoming a pro. The con was sleeping with strange men.

Bobbi laughed too. "It was a very fleeting impulse. Speaking of professionals, has Wes ever told you what George does for a living?"

"Not really. I kind of gathered he was into real estate. He talks about the housing market a lot, like he knows what going on."

Pulled over in a spot down the street, the girls continued to watch the scene. "Shit! Kandi... Look who just pulled into the garage and left his car too." Bobbi swung to Kandi, her voice cranky as shit and her eyes blazing mad. "What the fuck is Wes doing here?'

Kandi felt her face drop. She couldn't look at the woman next to her, not while swallowing the lump that had gathered and blinking away tears of disillusionment.

Bobbi, not one to wait for long, forced her chin up and snapped, "Okay, girlfriend, what the *fuck* is going on?"

Chapter Sixty-two

Dan didn't want Kandi to sense his relief when she'd cut their date short. If she hadn't, he would have had to. And the thought had been eating at him as to how he could do so without lying.

Saying it was work-related might have gotten him past her curiosity but it could also have initiated questions he didn't want to answer.

Earlier, Wes had cornered him in the men's room and let loose.

"That prick *has* been playing me. I didn't believe it at first when you told me he'd been accessing my data. But now, there's no doubt. I saw him."

"We didn't actually know how he pulled it off until you admitted to spending a boys' night with him most weeks. You were the one who figured it had to be through your phone. And you were right."

Dan smashed open the door of one of the toilet cubicles. The reverberating noise echoed in the empty room. "Son-of-bitchin' prick, I would have sworn on everything that's holy, he'd never do anything to hurt me or my family. Hell, when we were growing up, it was him who defended me against the big bad guys, made me want to be strong, help others too. He's probably why I'm an agent today. Fuck, when he showed up in my life last year, after an absence of ten years, I was thrilled. The bastard!"

Dan didn't know the mild-mannered man could be so dangerous until he'd erupted. Unknown to everyone but him and Wes, earlier they'd had the SWAT team set up numerous hidden cameras around the room and they had no doubt that George's switch would be easily visible on screen.

When Dan had first confronted Wes about their suspicions, back on the day that Kandi had been taken by Sam Dixon, he'd taken a chance and actually confided in Wes that he was under investigation.

Spurred on by Kandi's solid belief in her partner and the agent's professional behavior since he'd arrived, Dan became convinced of Wes's innocence. It was Wes who'd suggested he could be used as a decoy, and they'd hatched up a quick plan.

Dan couldn't believe that anyone who cared so much for his partners, and who would lay his life on the line to save them, could be guilty of the nefarious crap that the Cortés gang had been involved in recently.

Right now, some of the gang's members were suspected of more than one murder. Drugs flooding the streets were being attributed to the same manufacturer. In fact, they were identical to the last batch they'd intercepted from Mexico. And according to their sources, more shipments were being negotiated at that very moment. Ones they had no idea of their scheduled arrival, when or where. These pricks needed to be stopped before more lives were ruined.

After they'd set up George tonight, and Wes was convinced of his duplicity, the plan was simple. Wes would confront him.

Dan only hoped that Wes knew his friend as well as he seemed to think he did. If not, his life was on the line.

Chapter Sixty-three

"Bobbi, I think Wes is involved in something way over his head. After Dan mentioned the Cortés gang in conjunction with George Lewis, I did a search on that asshole. It turns out that around four years ago he began showing up and using the name Jorge Lobo"

"Wait, isn't Jorge Lobo now one of the top guys in the Cortés gang? They were trying to indict him on that big money-laundering scheme a while ago in Los Angeles, but he got off."

"Turns out, he's the same man. "

"Hell! Does Wes even know?"

"I'm not sure." Kandi didn't want to reveal everything she'd been told in confidence, but keeping back any information ate away at her.

Bobbi had been her partner for years, but Dan had been in enough trouble with the brass. She couldn't take the chance of anything she said or did being used as more ammunition against the man she adored.

Bobbi's eyes bored a hole in her conscience, but she didn't flinch. "You're not telling me everything, Kandicane. Let me guess. Some idiots are thinking that Wes is in on it, belongs to the gang. Hell, no one has ever seen Cortés. Are they thinking he's our chubby, curly-headed partner?" The laughter faded when Kandi didn't join in. "Get the fuck outta here! Kandi we're talking about Wes. Look at me."

Bobbi forced Kandi's chin to the left. The headlights of an approaching car lit up their darkened parking spot and Kandi saw the horror on her partner's face. "You believe it! Give your head a shake, Kandice Warner. It's Wes we're talking about here—new daddy-to-be, Wes."

Kandi wrenched her face away and sniffed. "Quit preaching to the converted. A while ago, I would have given everything I own in support of our guy. But tonight I saw it with my own eyes. He left his phone on the table on purpose—"

"Shit, girlfriend, he's always leaving his phone lying around."

"But tonight, George took it, and soon after he went to the bathroom. Came back and returned Wes's phone without anyone else seeing it, or should I say anyone but Wes. He knew it was happening and let it. I saw the whole thing." Cutting off the sob, she repeated, "I watched it happen."

Bobbi's face fell, and she clutched the steering wheel, yanking it viciously. Suddenly she swung around. "It makes no sense. George just up and makes off with Wes's phone and no one notices?"

"Because he had a decoy, a phone exactly the same as Wes's, right down to the perfect cover. The switch took less than a second and, as far as anyone else was concerned, it had been there the whole time."

"Well, that explains it. Wes's been fooled too."

"No. I watched Wes's reaction when George made the swap. He knew, but he did nothing. Trust me, Bobbi. Wes knew. The bastard knew."

"Aw, shit! You're breaking my heart. Goddamn him to hell. We trusted him. He's one of the good guys."

"I know. That's why I'm positive there has to be another explanation."

Her face clearing, Bobbi nodded. "That's why we're here tonight."

"Yep! I wanted to follow George and see if we could catch him associating with any of the known criminals who have a warrant out for their arrest. Maybe if we try shaking him down, we can find out what his game is."

"Okay, I'm with you. Let's go. Hold it!" Bobbi

hesitated before opening the door. "What do we say if George or Wes sees us there before we're ready to make our move?"

"We'll look shocked to see them and explain you got a call from an old friend, and she wanted us to meet with her here."

"Perfect. Who?"

"How about Alexia Foreman? She kept in touch and is doing really well now. I think her and Pat Wagner—you know Kevin's father, one of the hostages at the bank—seem to be keeping company now. But we can say she called and wanted a meeting. That she had some inside information about the Dixon brothers she never shared."

"Brilliant. Let's go. And, chickie, keep your eyes open. No telling what could happen in there if they make us for agents."

Chapter
Sixty-four

Getting past the doorman was a breeze with Bobbi's bullshit and the big black man's admiration for her curvy body. When they stepped into the place, it was like one would imagine, a glitzy joint trying to look high-end.

Loud piped-in music, rounded booths with tacky black leather seats and pretty people everywhere; some were dancing, others just schmoozing. Track lighting that left one blinded with only enough ability to see furniture but not faces unless within inches of them. And a curved bar totally loaded with mirrors, fancy bottles of all kinds, numerous sized glasses and blue neon rope lighting to set it off.

Making their way over to where one of the idle

bartenders stood, they ordered martinis and surveyed the crowd. Within minutes, Kandi moved over for a tall, gorgeous redhead and her shorter, black-haired friend. Both girls were dressed in silky, very short, slinky styles, looking as if they'd poured their bodies into the material. Not kind to bulges, neither of their dresses did them justice.

"Jorge's in a piss-poor mood tonight. He bruised my arm pushing me from the party room. I'm pissed at him, big time."

"Yeah, what was his all-fired hurry? Some guy shows up, and we're forced to get out."

"Probably just as well. I've seen Jorge when he's mad, but tonight he was livid. Almost felt sorry for the schmuck who set him off." The two got their drinks and moved off.

Kandi whispered to Bobbi, "Did you hear that?"

"Yep. I only have one question. Where's the party room?"

The bartender stepped forward. "You ladies looking for the party? It's around behind the bar, big glass door on the left. You can't miss it."

"Thanks, honey." Bobbi winked, picked up her glass and gestured to Kandi to follow. "We're on!"

Following directions, the girls acted nonchalant, as if they had all the right in the world being where they were. Finally arriving at the heavy glass door, Bobbi reached out and shoved it open a few inches. Before they could step into the room, Kandi heard the commotion.

"You're not supposed to come here, Wes. Someone could have made you for an agent and forced my hand."

"I had to come and tell you the game is up. They're onto me. Tonight has to be the night. Black suspects what's been going on."

Bobbi stiffened and her stare speared Kandi right through her kind heart and into a belly that had suddenly turned to ice.

See! I told you. Something's up. Being partners for so long meant they didn't need words. Sometimes looks spoke louder.

Bobbi lifted her finger to her mouth and both girls leaned in to listen again.

"Did you tell him anything?"

"How can I? I don't know it all. Plus, it's too dangerous. You need to get this last job seen to. I can't cover for you anymore."

Suddenly, a male arm reached out between the two interlopers and pulled the door closed, cutting off their spying. "Why the hell are you two broads listening at the door? How come you're sneaking around back here?" A security type, all brawn and no brains, questioned them, the sweat on his bald head glistened in the hallway light.

"We were told this was the party room, honey." Bobbi looked indignant. "We came ready to have a good time, and all we see are two dudes arguing and cussin'. No fun here. I'm going back to get me another drink. Come on, Cupcake."

"Nope, I don't think so. I figure you'd better come with me." He reached for Bobbi's arm and, instead, encountered Kandi's fist in his solar plexus. Gasping for breath, pissed now, he lunged for the retreating girls and missed. But the other two coming up the hall didn't. They had Kandi and Bobbi cornered.

George appeared suddenly from behind the glass doors. "What the fuck is going on out here?" His face underwent a huge change when he spotted Kandi and Bobbi. Eyes narrowing, his toothy grin replaced the anger of earlier and he spoke with less fury. "Shit me, if it isn't my girlfriends arriving early." He reached out to Kandi. "Come in, baby doll. We're ready for you." He led her toward him, and Bobbi shook off the guards, gave them a flippant grin and followed the other two.

"I don't think so." A tall man rounded the corner, and the whole world stopped. Kandi heard one of the guards whisper, his tone incredulous, "*Señor Cortés.*"

Kandi couldn't believe her eyes. She heard Bobbi's indrawn breath and knew she shared her horror. God! How gullible they'd been.

All this time, the culprit had been right there in front of them. How could he have fooled them this badly?

Chapter
Sixty-five

Neil Ware, their old boss, the man Dan had replaced, stepped toward them. He and his two bodyguards blocked the hallway, making escape impossible.

Bobbi spoke, her tone disparaging "Guess retirement wasn't exciting enough for you, boss. What? You get bored?"

Kandi stood, glued to the floor. Though she'd never had the kind of relationship with this man she'd enjoyed with others in the office, she'd looked up to him with respect. And he'd treated her in the same fashion.

In fact, many had hinted that he'd indulged Kandi, had had more time for her and given her a lot more leeway to do her job. Even had gone as far as making veiled references to the man having a crush on her, which had made her laugh and argue. *"For heaven's sake, Neil's old enough to be my father. He just looks after his own. You can't attack the man for caring about his team."*

Wes's usual reply had been made jokingly, *"Yeah, his blond haired, blue-eyed, Barbie-doll team member, maybe. With the rest of us, he's hard as nails and meaner than a snake with its ass caught in barbed wire."*

Now Neil faced them down with a nonchalance that brought quivers of distaste rushing through Kandi's whole body. This man had no fear. and if it were true that he was *Senor* Cortés, it was no wonder that the gang had thrived for years, always just under the radar. Having an inside knowledge of every move the authorities were making had most likely been invaluable to them getting away with... well, with murder.

"I'm sorry you showed up, Kandi. I have no idea why you're here, but I'm afraid we won't be able to let you go." Neil Ware spoke over his shoulder to one of the men there who merely looked bored. "Take their purses. We wouldn't want any surprises, like getting pepper spray in the face." His smirk made her wish she had the item in her hand.

The tall, black-suited man stepped around his boss and yanked both the girls' bags away from them. He checked inside, and when he pulled out their weapons a mean grin appeared. Then he retreated, but not before taking the liberty of letting his eyes roam over Bobbi's voluptuous frame.

Bobbi's scoffing sound had Neil turning her way. Her tone revealed her dislike. "Guess that includes me too, huh, Neil?"

"What includes you?"

"Not being happy to see me."

Neil's sudden grin wasn't at all pleasant. "Oh, Carter, I've never been happy to see you. In fact, I couldn't care less. You simply don't matter. Now, after you." He gestured for them to enter the playroom. "Jorge, shall we entertain our guests until the van arrives. Soon, they'll be taking a little trip into the mountains, and even the best search teams won't be able to find their remains."

George started to open the door and then stopped. "Sure, boss. And may I say, it's good to finally meet you in person. I'll get the ball rolling with their transport."

"All taken care of. Mendes will be here in a few minutes."

George's eyes widened. "He's back in town? I thought you wanted him to stay low after the last hit. He's a maniac, boss. Likes it rough and dirty."

Neil managed to appear slightly sorry over this dilemma. "True. But he gets the job done, and right now I can't afford any more mistakes. We need that final drug shipment, and since you managed to get the coordinates that the FBI figures we'll use, we'll be able to change them so the drugs will get through this time. We can't afford another screw-up like the last one. Once it's in the bag, we can split it, pay off the boys and then my retirement can start for real." Neil waved at the door. "Let's go. I want a whiskey."

They entered the room. George went first and held the door open. The two girls followed him, then Neil, his security guy and the bodyguards went in last.

Chapter
Sixty-six

Kandi held her breath as she stepped past the doorway. Wes waited until everyone had entered and George started to close the door before he made an appearance, his gun not wavering and his demeanor that of a man who wouldn't hesitate to shoot.

"Everyone up against the wall! Neil, you old bastard, get over there too. I want to see your hands. George, you get the guns and put them on the desk."

George, get the guns? Kandi had prayed for this result. She'd known Wes had been in the room, and now they had proof he was on their side after all. He was one of the good guys. But why in the hell was he giving George access to the guns?

"Wes, be careful. George is one of them. Don't trust him."

"Actually, he and I are partners. It's a long story, Cupcake. Wanna give him a hand and get these guys unarmed. I'll feel a whole lot better when I know we have all the weapons."

Still unsure, she watched as George patted down the security man, giving him a push when he showed signs of putting up a fight.

Shrugging, trusting Wes, Kandi began frisking the man who'd given Bobbi a hard time a few seconds earlier, and she wasn't gentle with the asshole either. "Get up against the wall and keep those hands up or so help me God, I'll dig my four-inch heel up your ass and enjoy hearing your screams."

"Way to go, girl!" Wes didn't hold back, and even Bobbi's laughter rang clearly. Bobbi and Wes shared a high-five as was their habit, and George ground out his discomfort. "Hey, quit goofing around. These guys don't play games."

In minutes, Bobbi, Kandi and George had emptied the other four of their weapons. "Want me to call for backup?" Kandi reached for her purse.

Wes grinned. "They're on their way. Be here in a few seconds."

Kandi, with her back turned to the men against the wall, didn't see the bodyguard move. But when hard hands bit into her skin, trying to haul her towards him, she reacted automatically.

Grabbing his arm in a firm grip, she wheeled, bent and, using her hip, flipped the fool onto the floor in front of her. Before she could follow through with a punch to the creep's throat, the door burst open and Dan led his men into the room.

He stopped dead when he saw her on the floor, leaning over a victim, her hand raised to deliver the final blow.

"Dammit, Kandi! Seriously? Again?"

Caught in the act, she looked up with a grin for the man who she loved ridiculously, wholeheartedly. "Danny, are you always going to spoil my fun?"

Chapter Sixty-seven

Dan had his men take control of the room, and in seconds they were leading the criminals away in handcuffs. All but George...

Kandi and Bobbi looked at each other, unanswered questions overlaying their expressions. They both cornered Wes, and Kandi hugged his arm. He squeezed her hand to his side and looked at them both fondly.

"Bobbi and I couldn't believe you were involved, Wes. But you sure had us fooled when you showed up here tonight."

"You think I had you fooled? What the hell were you two doing impeding the investigation?"

Bobbi piped up. "Kandi saw the phone exchange at the restaurant, so we decided to take a closer look at George's activities. Thinking he might be Cortés, we were going to do a bit of surveillance and see if any suspects might be here who we could pump for information. Little did we expect you to show up."

Wes grinned. "It must have looked bad. For both me and George. Who by the way is not really the man you think he is."

"Come on, Wes. Are you telling us he's neither Jorge Lobo nor George Lewis?"

Dan came over and moved in behind Kandi, but he didn't touch her. It worried her, and for some crazy reason, she sensed a problem, a coldness, and hesitated to make the first move.

"Detective George Lewis has been working undercover for the Narcotics Enforcement Administration for the Seattle PD and the DEA. Wes just informed me tonight when he called for backup."

George added. "I've been on this case for almost four years, infiltrating myself into the gang and working my way up the so-called corporate ladder."

Wes added. "When he moved back to Seattle, he went right into the undercover world, but he led me to believe he'd gone into property management. It was only recently when he suspected that Neil Low might be Cortés that he came to me for help."

Bobbi looked confused. "Hold it. Neil worked in our department and had access to all the files. He must have been using that knowledge to help get the drugs through FBI barriers."

Dan answered. "Sure. Whenever we'd get messages from our own undercover agents that the drug drones would be landing at a certain place, someone would send word at the last minute to change the GPS. We'd set up our net and come away empty-handed. It happened enough times that we knew one of our own people was accessing FBI files and sharing the data. For a time, we thought maybe it was Wes. Patti's uncle is my boss, Director Bob Mires, and when the word got to him, he became worried for his niece and talked me into coming back to Seattle, taking Neil's now empty position and snooping around. "

Kandi turned to face him. "You weren't disgraced in Washington and given this position as a way to get you out of town, were you?"

"Nope! Just doing a favor for a friend who happens to be my boss. The man's been a mentor to me for years, and I'd lay down my life for him. Taking on this assignment was a very small way for me to repay him what I owe." Dan looked over at Wes and smiled. "Though I have to admit, as soon as I met Wes, spying on him didn't sit right with me. And once I could see how much both you and Bobbi respected the man, well... let's just say, though the evidence convicted, I didn't believe it."

Wes added, "He sat me down and let me in on what everyone suspected, but I had to act dumb until I got a chance to warn George. When Dan orchestrated the goings-on tonight, I couldn't reach George to let him know the gig was up. I had no choice but to agree to let them set up the cameras."

"You knew about George."

"Yeah. Shortly after Neil retired, George opened up to me. Said they'd suspected Neil of hacking into my browser and accessing the intelligence he'd been using."

Bobbi snorted. "And we always thought the man was technologically inept."

George added, "After Neil retired, something happened, and we couldn't go through Wes's browser anymore. Unfortunately, Neil found out about our earlier relationship and forced me to hang out with Wes, learn his new password, then target his phone."

Bobbi piped up. "I don't get it. Once you knew about Neil, why didn't you just arrest him and break up the gang?"

George smiled. "Because we had no evidence that he was actually the main man. And it was Cortés we wanted. Though we suspected Cortés and Neil might be one and the same, we had no proof until Neil himself appeared tonight. And without Wes's help, we might never have been able to catch him at all."

They all turned to Wes who looked a bit sheepish. As he pushed up his glasses and took his time to reply, he scanned each face. "Okay, this is what we figure. About the time Neil left, I'd found out about the baby and changed my password which hadn't been done in a long time."

Bobbi hooted. "I bet it was something to do with Wesley Junior or Daddy-to-be."

Wes looked sheepish. "Something like that. Obviously, when they couldn't break in anymore, Neil was furious."

Nodding, Bobbi added, "The drug squad had put the kibosh to their last few shipments. I remember how happy everyone was." She looked at Kandi. "Remember?"

"Uh, huh. The whole office was stoked to see FBI efforts were being rewarded."

George grimaced. "While you were celebrating, Cortés—Neil—was in hot water up to his ears with the locals. He needed those drugs to get through."

Wes added, "George came to me with the scheme for the restaurant, where we switched phones so he could get the coordinates and pass them on."

"How would that draw out Cortés?" Kandi had to ask.

"George knew Neil had to have that information. Pretending it was too dangerous to pass it through regular channels, especially after the last few shipments had been intercepted, he refused to give it to anyone but the boss himself. This way, we could finally draw him into the open and find out the identity of the man who no one knew for sure."

"Ah... so tonight was the big meet."

George nodded. "It had to be. Things had boiled over for us too. With two undercover cops dead, we couldn't afford to let this last shipment clear. The gangs had planned on doubling up to compensate for the drugs they'd lost, and it had to be stopped. We needed to keep it off the streets. It was tonight or never."

Bobbi straightened after perching on the desk. "And we almost ruined it for you. Sorry, boys. But that oughta teach you a lesson."

Dan looked to George, who shook his head. Then he checked out Wes, who only wore a grin from ear to ear but refused to fall into her trap. Finally, he answered. "I know I'm going to regret asking, but what do you mean?"

"Well, it's as plain as the nose on your face. When shit is going down, Kandi and I are going to sniff it out every time. So why bother trying to cover it up. We're just too fucking smart for you boys."

Chapter Sixty-eight

Kandi laughed same as everyone else. But something was wrong, and she'd sensed it right from the time Dan had broken into the room. He refused to meet her eyes no matter how many times she'd tried to catch his. Earlier, he'd stood close, yes, but without touching her. And... his whole demeanor was that of a man facing a firing squad.

Not good, Kandi!

She'd only been dumped once. By a man who'd declared his love in one sentence and an ultimatum in the next. He'd loved her wholeheartedly but... hadn't been able to take her career, the danger and uncertainty. Besides going into detail about his fears, rather than trying to work something out, he'd put their budding relationship on the table....

it's either me or your job.

No discussion, no reasoning, total acquiescence on her part or nothing. Glad to have seen that side of the idiot's closed mind before they'd taken things any further, she'd told him not to let the door hit his stupid ass on the way out.

Until now, she'd put up solid barriers and protected herself from being hurt again. With Dan, all her guards had dropped, her normal reserve had been breached and if he left town without declaring himself, she wouldn't survive.

Face it, kiddo, he'll be leaving. The party's over. You'll be alone—again!

Now with the case having been solved, Wes vindicated and the office no longer under suspicion, it only made sense that Dan would be returning to his position in Washington. He'd be leaving Seattle, leaving her and taking her poor wretched heart with him.

Unable to join in with the others any longer, face them and pretend, she gathered her belongings and headed for the door.

Silence echoed eerily and seconds later, Dan stood by her side, took her arm in his and said in a very gentle voice. "I'll take you home now, Agent Warner."

"No!" She yanked her arm from his and backed up a step. "You need to stay and oversee the arrests, make sure that nothing's forgotten. I'll get a ride with Bobbi or take a taxi."

Suddenly Bobbi appeared at her side, and though her eyes questioned the sudden change, all she said was, "I'll give you a ride, sweets." Opening the door, she let Kandi pass through first.

***

Dan's touch stopped Bobbi, and though he never spoke, the question was totally visible to anyone who could read body language. And she was a whiz. *"What happened? Why'd she turn so moody all of a sudden?"*

Not answering with words, she shrugged, and the look in her eyes showed her concern. *Something's terribly wrong.*

He chewed his lip and rubbed at the twitching on his cheek. The spasms had never been this bad before, but then, he'd never faced such a son-of-a-bitchin' predicament before either. What the fuck was he going to do?

Now that Kandi was back in his life, he couldn't give her up—ever. The world had become a place he loved to wake up to every morning. The sun shone brighter, the air tasted better, even the trees and flowers had more essence, more beauty.

But the thought of living with the nightmarish terror his gorgeous lady had put him through over the last few weeks was also unbearable.

Seeing her in action tonight had scared the fucking daylights outta him. His dainty Kandi leaning over to land a blow on a man twice her size, a dude who could kill her with one punch...

Goddammit!

Just thinking about the danger had the bile rising and his stomach reacting like it had ever since he'd hit this crazy city. Never before had he agonized over every move a woman made. But now, it was like a red-hot poker being shoved down his throat when he knew she was in danger, and he had no right... no fucking right to intrude.

After all, the lady was just doing her job.

Chapter Sixty-nine

"You gonna tell me what that was all about?" Bobbi didn't pull any punches when it came to getting at the truth. Breaking the deadly silence, she drove carefully, heading to Kandi's.

"What?" Without looking her way, Kandi tried playing dumb but didn't hold up much hope she'd get away with it.

"Don't give me that shit. You turning cold as ice and leaving the scene before anyone else. Usually, it's the opposite."

"There were others to take over. They didn't need us to hang around."

"True. But that still doesn't explain why you were all smiles; face lit up like a flaming candle one minute and empty as shit the next. I've never seen you like this before, cookie. You got me worried."

A sob broke loose, but Kandi tamped it down. *Not here. Not yet. Wait. Soon.*

"I'm tired, Bobbi. Tired of the shit we deal with every day. I just want to go home." Though she tried with everything she had inside, the last few words were soaking in a sob, her bottom lip was wobbling, and she knew the tears would have gushed if she hadn't kept blinking. "I just want to go home."

Kandi appreciated that Bobbi wanted to stay with her, but her partner respected that Kandi needed this time alone. Once she handed Kandi over to a waiting Blue, enthusiastic to see her until he too sensed a problem, she gave Kandi one last hug, whispered her affection and added, "Call me if you need me, Cupcake. I'll always be there for you."

As soon as the car pulled away, Kandi sank to her knees beside her furry friend and gave him a hug, her tears dripping onto the heat of his body. Licking wherever he could reach, his whining soothed her a little.

"Kandi, baby. What's happened?" Ben stepped out from the back of the house, his worry evident but his voice pacified like it always had.

"Oh, Dad." She reached for him, and his arms wrapped around her tightly.

"Okay, sweetheart, come with me. You can tell your ol' dad all about it. Remember, nothing's as bad when it's shared." Boosting her to a standing position, he guided her into the house, to the living room where he lowered her to the sofa and then dropped beside her.

Those words had always soothed her while growing up but somehow, tonight, they didn't work. How could they? Dan would leave her. She'd be empty. And the world would be bleak.

"I can't talk about it. I just can't."

"Did something happen on the job?"

"Have you been here all along?"

Going along with her subject change, he winked. "You want the truth? Nothing but the truth."

"Yes." She sniffed and cuddled close.

"I've been hiding out in the back part of the house. I couldn't leave you again right away. Your old dad's having a hard time keeping his cool over your dangerous activities lately. I promised I'd never put any pressure on you over the job. But you gotta loosen the barriers and cut me some slack too."

She pulled from his arms, surprised to find them sitting together on the sofa. "I'm sorry I put you through so much, Dad. It never used to seem so dangerous, but lately..." She breathed a huge sigh that ended in a sob.

"Lately, what?"

"It's all too much." The dam broke and she sobbed like a little girl. "It's just too... too much, Dad. People hurting each other, selling drugs to kids, putting money before family or honor or love. I'm beginning to wonder if there're any good guys left in this sorry world."

Ben stiffened. He hummed for a few seconds and then words broke out. "You listen here, little girl. Sure, there are bad people in the world. Lots of 'em. Scads. You and I have met people that don't give a damn about who they hurt, or what they do to make things shitty for others. But those aren't the ones you're out there busting your butt to save. It's the good guys. Right? The decent folks who have to rely on cops all over the world to keep them safe and make things right."

Kandi listened, knowing his words were true. She sniffed and reached for the tissue that had miraculously appeared in his hand. "Just so you know, popsicle, I understand what it took outta you to tell me that."

"God, Kandi. I'd give my left testicle for you to decide that law enforcement didn't cut it for you anymore, or at least that an office position would work as well rather than being out in the field. But it has to be your decision, baby. As grim as I find it when you're in danger, you've been happy. And that's all a man can ask for his little girl."

Kandi flung herself into his arms and hugged tight. Before she could frame an answer, Blue ran toward her followed by a very nervous Dan. Timidity didn't suit the man, but he played the part perfectly, and discomfort enclosed all three of them.

Kandi had eyes now for only one person and Ben would have had to be a fool, a blind one at that, not to see it clearly. He patted her face, kissed her forehead and then stood. "I'll take Blue for a walk and leave you two alone."

Seeing the hunger on his daughter's face, he stopped beside Dan and whispered, making sure only the two of them could hear. "You keep that badge off of her and you'll have my total blessings. And if you can't, son, then you'd better keep her safe."

Chapter Seventy

Kandi straightened, tugging at her dress which had twisted. She used the tissue to wipe any evidence of her recent breakdown off her face. "I guess you came to say goodbye."

"Kandi, darlin', it's one o'clock in the morning. If I was going to say goodbye, I'd probably have waited until a reasonable hour." He swallowed, and she watched his nervousness turn him into a person so unlike her self-confident boss that she couldn't hold back the smile.

"Why are you grinning?" A spot of temper broke free and he rushed to her side. "Why weren't you happy earlier? You left, and I felt like shit."

She noticed that his blue silk tie, half mast, hung askew and his hair had been mussed repeatedly.

His hands were fisted and added to the look of a man at the end of his rope.

But mostly it was the twitching in his cheek that gave him away. Danny was suffering. It wasn't just her. Slowly, a notion took hold and once it settled in, she couldn't shake it loose.

"Why did you come?"

"Because you were unhappy."

"And that bothered you, why?"

"Because. You should never be unhappy. Not you. I love your smile too much to see the misery that replaced it tonight."

"You really do love me?"

"Of course! I adore you. It's always been you. Since I was a kid you were the only person who looked at me as if I mattered."

"Then why are you leaving me?"

"Who says I'm leaving you?" His voice had risen, and he glowered. "I'll never leave you."

"Then you're taking me with you?"

"Baby, only if you want to come with me. There're always openings in the bureau office there for top-notch female agents. But... if you don't want to leave here, I'll take on Ware's job permanently."

"That's a huge step down. You'd do that for me?"

"Of course. If you love it here, then you're happy here. We'll get married and live wherever you want."

She threw herself into his arms and wriggled

until she perched on his knee. "I'm happy wherever you are, love, and you're happy in D.C. But there's one thing I should mention."

He stopped nuzzling her neck and leaned back to see her eyes. "What's that?"

"I'm thinking that a mom shouldn't be in such a hazardous job as a federal agent. I'm thinking it's time for me to retire from the danger and maybe take on a less strenuous position."

He stiffened, his eyes widened, and he stuttered. "A mom?"

Nodding, she answered teasingly, "Uh, huh! It's my one ambition that I'd like to start working on as soon as possible. Is that okay?"

He shook her gently as if making his point couldn't be done with words alone. "Okay? It's the best news I've ever heard." An engaging smile, not seen since she'd last ridden a bus, appeared on Dan's face and her heart twisted inside.

My hero...

Afterword

Thank you so much for reading my book,
Special Agent Kandice.

I loved writing this story and I hope you enjoyed reading it. If so, I would ask you for a favor. Wherever you purchased this book, please take a few minutes and leave an honest review. Authors enjoy hearing that readers like their stories, and hopefully, others will see your words and choose to buy my work because of your kind sentiments.

My website at **http://mimibarbour.com** now has all my books listed with links to the venues to make it easy for you to return to where you bought the book and to find my other work.

While you're there, I'd really appreciate it if you would sign up for my newsletter so I can keep in touch. **http://bit.ly/mimibarbournewsletter**

I only send out newsletters approximately twice a month. It's usually full of giveaways, contests and freebies along with my personal news. (You have my word that your address will never be shared.)

Hugs, Mimi

Special
Agent
Maximilian

Undercover FBI Book #3

by
Mimi Barbour

NYT & USA Today Best-selling author

Identical twins but different men – she loves both.

In this electrifying romantic suspense set in the steamy streets of New Orleans, Lieutenant Commander Nik Baudin, accidently meets up with an identical twin he never knew existed. When his brother Max goes missing, Nik assumes his identity as Special Agent Maximilian. This gives him access to FBI files making it easier to arrest the gangsters who attacked his brother and to stop their trafficking of underage girls. Being that Nik has specialized commando training, he's the perfect man for the job – that's if his PTSD doesn't kick in and leave him cowering in a corner.

Special Agent Maya Barnes can't believe it when she spots her partner, Max Foster, wandering along the French market without a care in the world. Since he'd been beaten and had gone missing weeks earlier, they all believed him dead. There's only one problem... though this man might look exactly like the missing agent, she knows differently. In all the years they've worked together, she's never wanted to have mind-blowing sex with her partner before.

Praise and Reviews:

"Nik makes a good stand-in for Max. With a partner like Maya, he won't have a hard time. Max has found himself.... Shall we say... Indisposed! The characters are great. I enjoyed all the excitement and surprises, that continued throughout the book. The story was written so well, I didn't want to put the book down. I wanted to keep reading to see what was going to happen next, because I knew something was. This is a great series."

Reviewed by ~ Peggy Twigg

"I wish Ms. Barbour would write at least another dozen or more books in this vein. I loved every second of reading. The stories and characters are so real that I would really love to meet them. Thanks for all the fun and mystery. I appreciate it."

Reviewed by ~ Judy Robbins

Chapter One - Special Agent Maximilian

This bonus chapter, added for your pleasure, is another from the Undercover FBI series...

Chapter One

From the corner of his eye, Nik saw the redhead approaching, hair flying, face full of anger. He managed to duck in time to elude the fist aimed at his face, but the one that plowed into his belly caught him off guard.

"Maximilian Foster! Where the *hell* have you been? I've searched high and low for your sorry ass for more'n a month. Everyone thinks you're dead. And where do I find you? Sauntering in the French market as if you haven't a care in the world."

Imprisoning her wrists before she did major damage seemed to be the most intelligent thing for Nik to do, but he hadn't realized her skill. In seconds, she had him pinned to the wall of the shop next to where he stood—not wanting to hurt her, he'd let it happen.

"Lady, what the hell is wrong with you?" He stamped down on his rising frustration. *What's going on with this crazy dame?*

"What's wrong with me? *What's wrong with... are you kidding me?* We're partners, or have you forgotten that insignificant detail, and that it used to mean something?"

Ah! So, this was Max's partner, Maya Barnes. Now what the hell was he going to do? Recently, he'd made the decision to fake being his twin, pretend he was Max Foster. But maybe he'd gone and spoiled the chance. Thinking quickly, he attempted to recover lost ground.

"Maya? I'm sorry... I–I don't remember. I don't remember anything. I've been wandering around here praying something would be familiar. I'm sorry, I..." He choked on the word *sorry* since it wasn't a word he was familiar with, but he knew his brother used it a lot. That stupid word, along with his twin's winning smile, had no doubt gotten Max out of a lot of scrapes.

"Dammit, Max, don't try using that idiotic grin on me. You know it doesn't work. We've been hunting for you for weeks. One day you were there and the next you'd disappeared. I figured the Mosleys had gotten you once you'd let it out that we were on to them."

Mosleys? She had it half right. They had been after Max, and in the end, had put a hit on him. Only they weren't a local gang as the department thought. It went a lot deeper than just New Orleans bad boys. Seemingly, Max had clued into their operation, which had led back to Los Angeles. And it hadn't only been drugs. Nope! Things had gone deeper and dirtier than even he'd suspected.

Nik pretended a weakness he didn't feel and let his body slouch to the side. At first her green sparklers flared with suspicion, then softness flooded her expression and she supported rather than shoved.

"Oh God, Max. I'm sorry. You really are in a bad way, aren't you? Come on, let me help you. We'll grab a cup of coffee and you can tell me what happened."

Playing this lady while she was pissed hadn't bothered Nik whatsoever, but lying to her when those big eyes plied him with an affectionate pity was another thing altogether. What the hell was he to do now?

"I don't really want coffee, Maya. Maybe I could just come to the office."

Not taking his refusal seriously, Maya wrapped her arm around his body, clamped her fingers on his wrist and half dragged him through the open doors to a nearby table at Café du Monde. She led him to a seat and sat across from him. "Don't be silly, you love coffee. Look, you're a rotten son-of-a-bitch, but I'm glad to see you. I couldn't believe you'd leave me high and dry, worrying myself sick about what could have happened. Now it all makes sense."

Shaking his head, not understanding her logic, he just stared at her and waited. No doubt she'd enlighten him as to what she meant. He must have shown his lack of understanding because she assumed a disgusted look. "Stop being so dense! You might be a philandering S.O.B. and an unmitigated snob, but I'd never have believed you would treat me so shabbily. I guess I'm relieved to see I was right."

"You're relieved to know I can't remember anything? That I woke up in the ditch with a lump the size of an extra-large egg on the back of my head? God save me from trying to analyze the labyrinth of a female's mind."

Maya sat with her mouth open; her eyes focused and didn't utter a word. With a laser-like gaze, she drilled every spot of his face and then shook her head. "Even dressed like an army store reject, I'd swear you were Special Agent Maximilian Foster. Then you say something, and I have to admit to having huge doubts. And just so you know, Max'd die before appearing in public looking like G.I. Joe."

Nik had seconds to decide his future. To make up his mind if he was serious about going after the people who'd beaten his brother and left him broken, covered in blood and lying in a ditch. Guessing there had never really been a choice, he replied softly, "I'm sorry, Maya. You're the first person I've remembered, even remotely. That is, I know your name, but that's about it. You have to believe me when I tell you that I can't remember anything after being struck. My own clothes were covered in blood and I got these cheap. After all, I only had ten bucks in my pocket—no wallet, no I.D. I'm a mess, and I guess I need your help." Instinctively, watching the caring flood her face, he reached out his hand and she grasped his fingers and squeezed. Hard.

Her eyes, piercing green shards, speared him. "You lying piece of shit. I don't know what your game is, but you aren't, and never could be, Max. Now, who the hell are you and what's going on?"

***

If you've enjoyed this excerpt, you can purchase

the book here at Amazon.

Sweet
Retaliation

Mob Tracker Series, Book #1

Mimi Barbour
NYT & USA Today Best-selling author

*** *Warning: This is a series that must be read in*

order!!

A virgin librarian with hot-chick potential, the conflicts in her story won't let you put the book down. Be prepared for an all-nighter...

She watches the mob kill her twin and is too frozen with fear to stop them. How can she live with that cowardice eating away at her self-respect? Revenge claws at her sheltered existence until she can't breathe. Though she's naïve, she isn't stupid. When she finds a stash of loot in her brother's gym locker, she has the means.

Now all she needs is the guts to make every one of those low-life gang members pay.

People might think detectives are hard-assed cops with no home life, but Trace McGuire has a dying mom he loves fiercely. Already stressed over his personal problems, he takes a bullet for a virgin beauty hiding while mobsters shoot her brother.

This chick draws out every protective instinct he thought had disintegrated over years on the job and he becomes invested – in her hot body, her plans for retaliation and her fighting spirit.

Helpless, he watches her enter the seedy underworld that'll eat her alive.

Then he sees her fight.

And wonders if they'll survive her.

Praise and Reviews:

"I am in love with this book and I'll be following the series for more! Mimi Barbour did an awesome job!" ~ *Reviewed by Birna Bjornsdottir*

"Trace – oh Trace how I love you! As soon as he appeared in the story I knew I would fall in love with him and I did! He was a really great character, independent, focused and not afraid to push the limits when needed. Together he and Cass were amazing!

I really cannot wait to read more from this author in the future and highly recommend this story! You will have a hard time putting it down once you have started!" ~ *Reviewed by Katie_83*

"Ms. Barbour has written a gripping story about one woman's quest for justice. She has deftly created marvelous characters that pull you into their story. This is a suspense-filled, full-bore non-stop action ride that you will absolutely love." ~ *Reviewed by Colorado Avid Reader*

Chapter One - Sweet Retaliation

This bonus chapter added for your pleasure is Book #1 from my new popular series "The Mob Tracker."

***These books must be read in order.**

Chapter One

What the hell was she doing following her brother, especially at night? Cassidy Santino didn't do darkness. Not in the slums of a city like Las Vegas when, molasses thick, it threatened and terrified.

Gagging, sweating, she'd reached the end of her

backbone. Thoughts of giving up and retreating gobbled up the small amount of bravery still hanging on by a thread, making her hesitate. Then worry for her twin, Raoul, kicked in.

Biting her lip, she eased forward so she could see around the rickety fence into the semi-lit alley behind a big warehouse. A group of men milled about in a circle. Two of them were head-to-head in a heated discussion. Adrenalin kicked in when she saw her brother step out of the circle.

Raoul's shoulders were hunched in the same way he'd hold himself when their father had intimidated him as a boy. She watched him flinch and start to turn away. Then the man he'd been arguing with let out a bellow, backhanded him across the face and shoved hard. Before she could get her bewildered brain to accept the incident, Raoul went down and the other men crowded in and began kicking him.

No! Stop!

Her mind screamed the words, but her voice didn't connect. It froze. When she opened her mouth fear struck her mute. Though she tried to release her rage, to force sound past the blockage in her throat, not even a peep escaped. She'd never felt so useless in all her sad, ineffectual years. Forcing her limbs to move, she fell forward onto her knees but couldn't get her leg muscles to function.

Infuriating seconds ticked by as she watched the

men work her brother over like he was a soccer ball, rather than a human being.

God! Please...

Movement, shuffling, a voice called out from another direction. "Police. Stop what you're doing and back away. Get your hands up. Do it now!"

Thank you, Lord! Confidence arrived with the authorities, and Cassi felt a flood of energy. Springing to her feet, she started forward. Before she went two steps, one of the assailants stepped over to Raoul, extended his arm and a gunshot changed the rest of her life. She heard her twin grunt and saw his body jerk.

"No!"

Fear vanished under her instinctive urgency to get to Raoul. She ran. To help him, save him, give up her life for him. He was all she had in the world, the only one who mattered.

Blinded by grief, unaware of the loud gunplay going on around her, she fell to her knees next to his lifeless form. Before she had a chance to understand the danger, a man dashed out, swept her to the side and covered her with his own body.

"Keep down." Rough, his hands hurting, he pushed her head under his chest while she wiggled to get back to Raoul. "Stop it. You'll get us both killed." His voice, hard and angry drew her attention. She shook away from his hand and looked at him, trying to explain that the injured man was her brother and he needed help. When their eyes met, the bit of light from the building's illumination revealed his face.

Deep blue eyes, encircled with a dark outer ring of pure determination, penetrated for an instant, an order clear and visible that only a man in command could produce. Compelled to obey, but overridden by her need to get to Raoul, she kept pushing at him, until she felt him jerk and heard his grunt of pain.

One of those monsters had shot her rescuer. Disbelief overwhelmed and in seconds the relentless fear returned. Imprisoned and helpless, the horror of the moment clawed at her sanity. Surrendering to its magnetic lure, darkness claimed her and she knew no more.

****

If you've enjoyed this excerpt, you can purchase the book here at **AMAZON**

A word about the author, Mimi Barbour

MIMI BARBOUR: New York Times & USA Today Best-selling, award-winning romance author has written seven series, many single-tiles and is involved in a huge number of box collections.

She lives on the beautiful East coast of Vancouver Island and writes her books with tongue-in-cheek and a mad glint in her eye. The fans all agree that it's the fascinating characters she creates which makes her writing so entertaining and brings them back for more of her magic.

"The favorite part of my job is meeting the characters from each new book. Designing them the way I want and having them act however I think they should. It's thrilling, especially when most of my make-believe folks are people I would love to interact with in reality."

Contact me:

Amazon author page: http://bit.ly/
MimiBarbourAmazon

My website: http://www.mimibarbour.com/

Or follow me on twitter: https://twitter.com/
MimiBarbour

Or on Facebook: Mimi Barbour Fan page

Please sign up for my fun Newsletter: http://bit.ly/
mimibarbournewsletter
or

Write to me anytime. I love to hear from my
readers... xo
mailto:mimibarbour66@gmail.com